"You've hated every minute of it, haven't you, Radinck?

"But I'm going to my room in a few minutes, only before I go, I'd like to thank you for giving me such a nice wedding." She added kindly, "It's only this one evening, you know, you won't have to do it ever again. You asked me not to disturb your life, and I won't, only they all expected..." She pinkened faintly. "Well, they expected us to look—like..."

"Exactly, Caroline." He had got to his feet. "I'm only sorry that I didn't think of the wedding cake." He smiled at her: it was a kind, gentle sort of smile and it held a touch of impatience. She said good night without fuss and didn't linger. She thought about that smile later, as she got ready for bed. It had been a glimpse of Radinck again, only next time, she promised herself, he would smile without impatience. It might take a long time, but that was something she had.

Romance readers around the world were sad to note the passing of **Betty Neels** in June 2001. Her career spanned thirty years, and she continued to write into her ninetieth year. To her millions of fans, Betty epitomized the romance writer, and yet she began writing almost by accident. She had retired from nursing, but her inquiring mind still sought stimulation. Her new career was born when she heard a lady in her local library bemoaning the lack of good romance novels. Betty's first book, *Sister Peters in Amsterdam,* was published in 1969, and she eventually completed 134 books. Her novels offer a reassuring warmth that was very much a part of her own personality. She was a wonderful writer, and she will be greatly missed. Her spirit and genuine talent will live on in all her stories.

THE BEST *of*

BETTY NEELS

CAROLINE'S WATERLOO

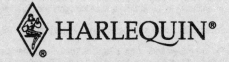

HARLEQUIN®

TORONTO • NEW YORK • LONDON
AMSTERDAM • PARIS • SYDNEY • HAMBURG
STOCKHOLM • ATHENS • TOKYO • MILAN • MADRID
PRAGUE • WARSAW • BUDAPEST • AUCKLAND

ISBN 0-373-81117-9

CAROLINE'S WATERLOO

Copyright © 1980 by Betty Neels.

This edition published by arrangement with Harlequin Books S.A.

® and TM are trademarks of the publisher. Trademarks indicated with
® are registered in the United States Patent and Trademark Office, the
Canadian Trade Marks Office and in other countries.

www.eHarlequin.com

Printed in U.S.A.

CHAPTER ONE

THE NARROW brick road wound itself along narrow canals, through wide stretches of water meadows and small clumps of trees and, here and there, a larger copse. Standing well away from the road there were big farmhouses, each backed by a great barn, their mellow red brick glistening in the last rays of the October sun. Save for the cows, already in their winter coats, and one or two great horses, there was little to be seen and the only other movement was made by the four girls cycling briskly along the road. They had come quite a distance that day and now they were flagging a little; the camping equipment each carried made it heavy going, and besides, they had lost their way.

It had been easy enough leaving Alkmaar that morning, going over the Afsluitdijk and into Friesland, pedalling cheerfully towards the camping ground they had decided upon, but now, with no village in sight and the dusk beginning to creep over the wide Friesian sky, they were getting uneasy.

Presently they came to a halt, to look at the map and wonder where they had gone wrong. 'This doesn't go anywhere,' grumbled the obvious leader, a tall, very pretty girl. 'What shall we do? Go back— and that's miles—or press on?'

They all peered at the map again, one fair head, two dark ones and an unspectacular mouse-brown. The owner of the mouse-brown hair spoke:

'Well, the road must go somewhere, they wouldn't have built it just for fun, and we've been on it now for quite a while—I daresay we're nearer the end than the beginning.' She had a pretty voice, soft and slightly hesitant, perhaps as compensation for her very ordinary face.

Her three companions peered at the map again. 'You're right, Caro—let's go on before it's quite dark.' The speaker, one of the dark-haired girls, glanced around her at the empty landscape. 'It's lonely, isn't it? I mean, after all the towns and villages we've been through just lately.'

'Friesland and Groningen are sparsely populated,' said Caro, 'they're mostly agricultural.'

The three of them gave her a tolerant look. Caro was small and quiet and unassuming, but she was a fount of information about a great many things, because she read a lot, they imagined with a trace of pity;

unlike the other nurses at Oliver's, she was seldom invited to go out by any of the young doctors and she lived alone in a small bedsitter in a horrid shabby little street convenient to the hospital. She had any number of friends, because she could be relied upon to change off-duty at a moment's notice, lend anything needed without fuss, and fill in last-minute gaps. As she was doing now; the nurse who should have been in her place had developed an appendix and because four was a much better number with which to go camping and biking, she had been roped in at the last minute. She hadn't particularly wanted to go; she had planned to spend her two weeks' holiday redecorating her room and visiting art galleries. She knew almost nothing about art, but she had discovered long ago that art galleries were restful and pleasant and there were always other people strolling around for company, even though no one ever spoke to her. Not that she minded being alone; she had grown up in a lonely way. An orphan from childhood, the aunt she had lived with had married while Caro was still at school and her new uncle had never taken to her; indeed, over the years, he had let it be known that she must find a home for herself; her aunt's was too small to house all three of them. If she had been pretty he might have thought differently, and if she had tried to conciliate him he might have had second thoughts. As it was, Caroline hadn't seen her aunt for two years or more.

'Well, let's get on,' suggested Stacey. She tossed her blonde hair back over her shoulders and got on to her bike once more, followed by Clare and Miriam with Caro bringing up the rear.

The sun seemed to set very rapidly and once it had disappeared behind them, the sky darkened even more rapidly. But the road appeared to run ahead of them, clearly to be seen until it disappeared into a large clump of trees on the horizon. There were distant lights from the farmhouse now, a long way off, but they dispelled the loneliness so that they all became cheerful again, calling to and fro to each other, discussing what they would eat for their supper and whose turn it was to cook. They reached the trees a few minutes later, and Stacey, still in front, called out excitedly: 'I say, look there, on the left—those lights—there must be a house!' She braked to take a better look and Clare and Miriam, who hadn't braked fast enough, went into her, joined seconds later by Caro, quite unable to stop herself in time. She ploughed into the struggling heap in front of her, felt a sharp pain in her leg and then nothing more, because she had hit her head on an old-fashioned milestone beside the cycle path.

She came to with a simply shocking headache, a strange feeling that she was in a nightmare, and the pain in her leg rather worse. What was more, she was being carried, very awkwardly too, with someone supporting her legs and her head cradled against what felt like an alpaca jacket—but men didn't wear alpaca jackets any more. She tried to say so, but the words didn't come out right and she was further mystified by a man's cockney voice close to her ear, warning someone to go easy. She wanted to say, 'My leg hurts,' but talking had become difficult and when she made her eyes open, she could see nothing much; a small strip of sky between tall trees and somewhere ahead lights shining. She gave up and passed out again, unaware that the awkward little party had reached the house, that Stacey, obedient to the cockney voice, had opened the door and held it wide while the others carried her inside. She was unaware too of the size and magnificence of the hall or of its many doors, one of which was flung open with some force by a large man with a sheaf of papers in his hand and a scowl on his handsome features. But she was brought back to consciousness by his commanding voice, demanding harshly why he was forced to suffer such a commotion in his own house.

It seemed to Caro that someone should speak up and explain, but her head was still in a muddle although she knew what she wanted to say; it was just a question of getting the words out. She embarked on an explanation, only to be abruptly halted by the harsh voice, very close to her now. 'This girl's concussed and that leg needs attention. Noakes, carry her into the surgery.' She heard his sigh. 'I suppose I must attend to it.'

Just for a moment her addled brain cleared. She said quite clearly: 'You have no need to be quite so unfeeling. Give me a needle and thread and I'll do it myself.'

She heard his crack of laughter before she went back into limbo again.

She drifted in and out of sleep several times during the night and each time she opened her eyes it was to see, rather hazily, someone sitting by her bed. He took no notice of her at all, but wrote and read and wrote again, and something about his austere look convinced her that it was the owner of the voice who had declared that she was concussed.

'I'm not concussed,' she said aloud, and was surprised that her voice sounded so wobbly.

He had got to his feet without answering her, given her a drink and said in a voice which wasn't going to take no for an answer: 'Go to sleep.'

It seemed a good idea; she closed her eyes.

The next time she woke, although the room was dim she knew that it was day, for the reading lamp by the chair was out. The man had gone and Stacey sat there, reading a book.

'Hullo,' said Caro in a much stronger voice; her head still ached and so did her leg, but she had stopped feeling dreamlike.

Stacey got up and came over to the bed. 'Caro, do you feel better? You gave us all a fright, I can tell you!'

Caro looked carefully round the room, trying not to move her head because of the pain. It was a splendid apartment, its walls hung with pale silk, its rosewood furniture shining with age and polishing. The bed she was in had a draped canopy and a silken bedspread, its beauty rather marred by the cradle beneath it, guarding her injured leg.

'What happened' she asked. 'There was a very cross man, wasn't there?'

Stacey giggled. 'Oh, ducky, you should have heard yourself! It's an enormous house and he's so good-looking you blink…'

Caroline closed her eyes. 'What happened?'

'We all fell over, and you cut your leg open on Clare's pedal—it whizzed round and gashed it badly, and you fell on to one of those milestones and knocked yourself out.'

'Are you all right? You and Clare and Miriam?'

'Absolutely, hardly a scratch between us—only you, Caro—we're ever so sorry.' She patted Caro's arm. 'I've got to tell Professor Thoe van Erckelens you're awake.'

Caro still had her eyes shut. 'What an extraordinary name…'

Her hand was picked up and her pulse taken and

she opened her eyes. Stacey had gone, the man—presumably the Professor—was there, towering over her.

He grunted to himself and then asked: 'What is your name, young lady?'

'Caroline Tripp.' She watched his stern mouth twitch at the corners; possibly her name sounded as strange to him as his did to her. 'I feel better, thank you.' She added, 'It was kind of you to sit with me last night.'

He had produced an ophthalmoscope from somewhere and was fitting it together. 'I am a doctor, Miss Tripp—a doctor's duty is to his patient.'

Unanswerable, especially with her head in such a muddled state. He examined her eyes with care and silently and then spoke to someone she couldn't see. 'I should like to examine the leg, please.'

It was Stacey who turned back the coverlet and removed the cradle before unwinding the bandage which covered Caro's leg from knee to ankle.

'Did you stitch it?' asked Caro, craning her neck to see.

A firm hand restrained her. 'You would be foolish to move your head too much,' she was told. 'Yes, I have cleaned and stitched the wound in your leg. It is a deep, jagged cut and you will have to rest it for some days.'

'Oh, I can't do that,' said Caro, still not quite in control of her woolly wits, 'I'm on duty in four days' time.'

'An impossibility—you will remain here until I consider you fit to return.'

'There must be a hospital…' Her head was beginning to throb.

'As a nurse you should be aware of the importance of resting both your brain and your leg. Kindly don't argue.'

She was feeling very peculiar again, rather as though she were lying in a mist, listening to people's voices but quite unable to focus them with her tired eyes. 'You can't possibly be married,' she mumbled, 'and you sound as though you hate me—you must be a mi—mi…'

'Misogynist.'

She had her eyes shut again so that she wouldn't cry. He was being very gentle, but her leg hurt dreadfully; she was going to tell him so, but she dropped off again.

Next time she woke up it was Clare by the bed and she grinned weakly and said: 'I feel better.'

'Good. Would you like a cup of tea?—it's real strong tea, like we make at Oliver's.'

It tasted lovely; drinking it, Caroline began to feel that everything was normal again. 'There's some very thin bread and butter,' suggested Clare. Caro devoured that too; she had barely swallowed the last morsel before she was asleep again.

It was late afternoon when she woke again. The

lamp was already lighted and the Professor was sitting beside it, writing. 'Don't you have any patients?' asked Caroline.

He glanced up from his writing. 'Yes. Would you like a drink?'

She had seen the tray with a glass and jug on it, on the table by her bed. 'Yes, please—I can help myself; I'm feeling fine.'

He took no notice at all but got up, put an arm behind her shoulders, lifted her very gently and held the glass for her. When she had finished he laid her down again and said: 'You may have your friends in for ten minutes,' and stalked quietly out of the room.

They crept in very silently and stood in a row at the foot of the bed, looking at her. 'You're better,' said Miriam, 'the Professor says so.' And then: 'We're going back tomorrow morning.'

Caro tried to sit up and was instantly thrust gently back on to her pillow. 'You can't—you can't leave me here! He doesn't like me—why can't I go to hospital if I've got to stay? How are you going?'

'Noakes—that's the sort of butler who was at the gate when we fell over—he's to drive us to the Hoek. The bikes are to be sent back later.'

'He's quite nice,' said Clare, 'the Professor, I mean—he's a bit terse but he's been a perfect host. I don't think he likes us much but then of course, he's quite old, quite forty, I should think; he's always reading or writing and he's away a lot—Noakes says he's a very important man in his profession.' She giggled, 'You can hardly hear that he's Dutch, his English is so good, and isn't it funny that Noakes comes from Paddington? but he's been here for years and years—he's married to the cook. There's a housekeeper too, very tall and looks severe but she's not.'

'And three maids besides a gardener,' chimed in Miriam. 'He must be awfully rich.'

'You'll be OK,' Stacey assured her, 'you'll be back in no time. Do you want us to do anything for you?'

Caro's head was aching again. 'Would you ask Mrs Hodge to go on feeding Waterloo until I get back? There's some money in my purse—will you take some so that she can get his food?'

'OK—we'll go round to your place and make sure he's all right. Do you have to pay Mrs Hodge any rent?'

'No, I pay in advance each month. Is there enough money for me to get back by boat?'

Stacey counted. 'Yes—it's only a single fare and I expect Noakes will take you to the boat.' She came a bit nearer. 'Well, 'bye for now, Caro. We hate leaving you, but there's nothing we can do about it.'

Caro managed a smile. 'I'll be fine—I'll let you know when I'm coming.'

They all shook hands with her rather solemnly. 'We're going quite early and the Professor said we weren't to disturb you in the morning.'

Caroline lay quietly after they had gone, too tired to feel much. Indeed, when the Professor came in later and gave her a sedative she made no demur but drank it down meekly and closed her eyes at once. It must have been quite strong because she was asleep at once, although he stayed for some time, sitting in his chair watching her, for once neither reading nor writing.

She didn't wake until quite late in the morning, to find Noakes' wife—Marta—standing by the bed with a small tray. There was tea again and paper-thin bread and butter and scrambled egg which she fed Caro with just as though she were a baby. She spoke a little English too, and Caro made out that her friends had gone.

When Marta had gone away, she lay and thought about it; she felt much more clear-headed now, almost herself, but not quite, otherwise she would never have conceived the idea of getting up, getting dressed, and leaving the house. She couldn't stay where she wasn't welcome—it was like her uncle all over again. Perhaps, she thought miserably, there was something about her that made her unacceptable as a guest. She was on the plain side, that she already knew, and perhaps because of that she was self-effacing and inclined to be shy. She had quickly learned not to draw attention to herself, but on the other hand she had plenty of spirit and a natural friendliness which had made her a great number of friends. But the Professor, she felt, was not one of their number.

The more she thought of her scheme, the more she liked it; the fact that she had a considerable fever made it seem both feasible and sensible, although it was neither. She began, very cautiously, to sit up. Her head ached worse than ever, but she ignored that and concentrated on moving her injured leg. It hurt a good deal more than she had expected, but she persevered until she was sitting untidily on the edge of the bed, her sound foot on the ground, its stricken fellow on its edge. It had hurt before; now, when she started to dangle it over the side of the bed, the pain brought great waves of nausea sweeping over her.

'Oh, God!' said Caro despairingly, and meant it.

'Perhaps I will do?' The Professor had come softly into the room, taking great strides to reach her.

'I'm going to be sick,' moaned Caro, and was, making a mess of his beautifully polished shoes. If she hadn't felt so ill she would have died of shame, as it was she burst into tears, sobbing and sniffing and gulping.

The Professor said nothing at all but picked her

up and laid her back in bed again, pulling the covers over her and arranging the cradle just so over her injured leg before getting a sponge and towel from the adjoining bathroom and wiping her face for her. She looked at him round the sponge and mumbled: 'Your shoes—your lovely shoes, I'm so s-sorry.' She gave a great gulp. 'I should have gone with the others.'

'Why were you getting out of bed?' He didn't sound angry, only interested.

'Well, I thought I could manage to dress and I've enough money, I think—I was going back to England.'

He went to the fireplace opposite the bed and pressed the brass wall bell beside it. When Noakes answered it he requested a clean pair of shoes and a tray of tea for two and waited patiently until these had been brought and Noakes, accompanied by a maid, had swiftly cleared up the mess. Only then did he say: 'And now suppose we have a little talk over our tea?'

He pulled a chair nearer the bed, handed her a cup of tea and poured one for himself. 'Let us understand each other, young lady.'

Caroline studied him over the rim of her cup. He talked like a professor, but he didn't look like one; he was enormous and she had always thought of professors as small bent gentlemen with bald heads and untidy moustaches, but Professor Thoe van Erckelens had plenty of hair, light brown, going grey, and cut short, and he had no need to hide his good looks behind a moustache. Caro thought wistfully that he was exactly the kind of man every girl hoped to meet one day and marry; which was a pity, because he obviously wasn't the marrying kind…

'If I might have your full attention?' enquired the Professor. 'You are sufficiently recovered to listen to me?'

Her head and her leg ached, but they were bearable. She nodded.

'If you could reconcile yourself to remaining here for another ten days, perhaps a fortnight, Miss Tripp? I can assure you that you are in no fit condition to do much at the moment. I shall remove the stitches from your leg in another four days and you may then walk a little with a stick, as from tomorrow, and provided your headache is lessening, you may sit up for a period of time. Feel free to ask for anything you want, my home is at your disposal. There is a library from which Noakes will fetch a selection of books, although I advise you not to read for a few days yet, and there is no reason why you should not sit in the garden, well wrapped up. You will drink no alcohol, nor will you smoke, and kindly refrain from watching television for a further day or so; it will merely aggravate your headache. I must ask you to excuse me from keeping you company at any time—I am a busy man and I have my work and my own interests.

I shall of course treat you as I would any other patient of mine and when I consider you fit to travel, I
will see that you get back safely to your home.'

Caro had listened to this precise speech with astonishment; she hadn't met anyone who talked like
that before—it was like reading the instructions on
the front of a medicine bottle. She loved the bit about
no drinking or smoking; she did neither, but she
wondered if she looked the kind of girl who did. But
one thing was very clear. The Professor was offer-
ing her hospitality but she was to keep out of his way;
he didn't want his ordered life disrupted—which
was amusing really; now if it had been Clare or
Stacey or Miriam, all pretty girls who had never
lacked for men friends, that would have been a different matter, but Caroline's own appearance was
hardly likely to cause even the smallest ripple on the
calm surface of his life.

'I'll do exactly as you say,' she told him, 'and I'll
keep out of your way—you won't know I'm here.
And thank you for being so kind.' She added: 'I'm
truly sorry about me being sick and your shoes...'

He stood up. 'Sickness is to be expected in cases
of concussion,' he told her. 'I am surprised that you,
a nurse, should not have thought of that. We must
make allowances for your cerebral condition.'

She looked at him helplessly. Underneath all that
pedantic talk there was a quite ordinary man; for

some reason, the professor was concealing him. After he had gone she lay back on her pillows, suddenly sleepy, but before she closed her eyes she decided that she would discover what had happened to make him like that. She must make friends with Noakes...

She made splendid progress. The Professor dressed her leg the next morning and when Marta had draped her in a dressing gown several sizes too large for her, he returned to lift her into a chair by the open window, for the weather was glorious and the view from it delightful. The gardens and the house were large and full of autumn colours, and just to lie back with Marta tucking a rug over her and settling her elevenses beside her was bliss. She had been careful to say very little to the Professor while he attended to her leg; he had made one or two routine remarks about the weather and how she felt and she had answered him with polite brevity, but now he had gone and despite his silence, she felt lonely. She sipped the warm milk Marta had left for her and looked at the view. The road was just visible beyond the grounds and part of the drive which led to it from the house; presently she heard a car leaving the house and caught a glimpse of it as it flashed down the drive: an Aston Martin—a Lagonda. The Professor must have a friend who liked fast driving. Caro thought that it might be rather fun to know someone who drove an Aston Martin, and even more fun to actually ride in one.

She was to achieve both of these ambitions. The Professor came as usual the following morning after breakfast to dress her leg, but instead of going away immediately as he usually did he spoke to Juffrouw Kropp who had accompanied him and then addressed himself to Caro.

'I am taking you to the hospital in Leeuwarden this morning. You are to have your head X-rayed. I am certain that no harm has come from your concussion, but I wish my opinion to be confirmed.'

Caro eyed him from the vast folds of her dressing gown. 'Like this?' she asked.

He raised thick arched brows. 'Why not? Juffrouw Kropp will assist you.' He had gone before she could answer him.

Juffrouw Kropp's severe face broke into a smile as the door closed. She fetched brush and comb and make-up and produced a length of ribbon from a pocket. She brushed Caro's hair despite her protests, plaited it carefully and fastened it with the ribbon, fetched a hand mirror and held it while Caro did things to her face, then fastened the dressing gown and tied it securely round Caro's small waist. Like a well-schooled actor, the Professor knocked on the door, just as though he had been given his cue, plucked Caro from the bed and carried her downstairs where Noakes stood, holding the front door wide. The Professor marched through with a muttered word and Noakes slid round him to open the door of the Aston Martin, and with no discomfort at all Caro found herself reclining on the back seat with Noakes covering her with a light rug and the Professor, to her astonishment, getting behind the wheel.

'This is never your car?' she asked, too surprised to be polite.

He turned his head and gave her an unfriendly look. 'Is there any reason why it shouldn't be?' he wanted to know, coldly.

She said kindly: 'You don't need to get annoyed. It's only that you don't look the kind of man to drive a fast car.' She added vaguely: 'A professor...'

'And no longer young,' he snapped. 'I have no interest in your opinions, Miss Tripp. May I suggest that you close your eyes and compose yourself—the journey will take fifteen minutes.'

Caroline did as she was bid, reflecting that until that very moment she hadn't realised what compelling eyes he had; slate blue and very bright. When she judged it safe, she opened her eyes again; she wasn't going to miss a second of the ride; it would be something to tell her friends when she got back. She couldn't see much of the road because the Professor took up so much of the front seat, but the telegraph poles were going past at a terrific rate; he

drove fast all right and very well, and he didn't slow
at all until she saw buildings on either side of them
and presently he was turning off the road and stopping smoothly.

He got out without speaking and a moment later
the door was opened and she was lifted out and set
in a wheelchair while the Professor spoke to a youngish man in a white coat. He turned on his heel without even glancing at her and walked away, into the
hospital, leaving her with the man in the white coat
and a porter.

How rude he is, thought Caro, and then: poor
man, he must be very unhappy.

She was wheeled briskly down a number of cor-
ridors to the X-ray department. It was a modern hospital and she admired it as they went, and after a
minute or so, when the white-coated man spoke
rather diffidently to her in English, showered him
with a host of questions. He hadn't answered half of
them by the time they reached their destination and
she interrupted him to ask: 'Who are you?'

He apologised. 'I'm sorry, I have not introduced
myself. Jan van Spaark—I am attached to Professor
Thoe van Erckelens' team. I am to look after you
while you are here.'

'A doctor?'

He nodded. 'Yes, I think you would call me a
medical registrar in your country.'

The X-ray only took a short while, and in no time at all she was being wheeled back to the entrance hall, but here, to her surprise, her new friend wished her goodbye and handed her over to a nurse, who offered a hand, saying: 'Mies Hoeversma—that is my name.'

Caro shook it. 'Caroline Tripp. What happens next?'

'You are to have coffee because Professor Thoe van Erckelens is not quite ready to leave.'

She was wheeled to a small room, rather gloomy and austerely furnished used, Mies told her, as a meeting place for visiting doctors, but the coffee was hot and delicious and Mies, although her English was sketchy, was a nice girl. Caro, who had been lonely even though she hadn't admitted it to herself, enjoyed herself. She could have spent the morning there, listening to Mies describing life in a Dutch hospital and giving her a lighthearted account of her own life in London, but the door opened, just as they had gone off into whoops of mirth over something or other, and the porter reappeared, spoke to Mies and wheeled Caro rapidly away, giving her barely a moment in which to say goodbye.

'Why the hurry?' asked Caro, hurriedly shaking hands again.

'The Professor—he must not be kept waiting.' Mies was quite serious; evidently he had the same effect on the hospital staff as he had on his staff at home. Instant, quiet obedience—and yet they liked him…

Caroline puzzled over that as she was whisked carefully to the car, to be lifted in by the Professor before he got behind the wheel and drove away. Jan van Spaark had been there, with two other younger men and a Sister, the Professor had lifted his hand in grave salute as he drove away.

He seemed intent on getting home as quickly as possible, driving very fast again, and it was a few minutes before Caroline ventured in a small polite voice: 'Was it all right—my head?'

'There is no injury to the skull,' she was assured with detached politeness. 'Tomorrow I shall remove the stitches from your leg and you may walk for brief periods—with a stick, of course. You will rest each afternoon and read for no more than an hour each day.'

'Very well, Professor, I'll do as you say.' She sounded so meek that he glanced at her through his driving mirror. When she smiled at him he looked away at once.

He carried her back to her room when they reached the house and set her down in the chair made ready for her by the window. 'After lunch I will carry you downstairs to one of the sitting rooms. Are you lonely?'

His question took her by surprise. She had her mouth open to say yes and remembered just in time that he wanted none of her company.

'Not in the least, thank you,' she told him. 'I live alone in London, you know—I have a flat, close to Oliver's.'

He nodded, wished her goodbye and went away—she heard the car roar away minutes later. Not a very successful morning, she considered, although he had wanted to know if she were lonely. And she had told a fib—not only was she lonely, but the flat she had mentioned so casually was in reality a bedsitter, a poky first floor room in a dingy street... She was reminded forcibly of it now and of dear old Waterloo, stoically waiting for her to come back. She longed for the sight of his round whiskered face and the comfort of his plump furry body curled on her knee. 'I'm a real old maid,' she said out loud, and then called, 'Come in,' in a bright, cheerful voice because there was someone at the door.

It was Noakes with more coffee. 'And the Professor says if yer've got an 'eadache, miss, yer ter take one of them pills in the red box.'

'I haven't got a headache, thank you, Noakes, not so's you'd notice. Has the Professor gone again?'

'Yes, miss—Groningen this time. In great demand, 'e is.'

'Yes. It's quiet here, isn't it? Doesn't he ever have guests or family?' Noakes hesitated and she said at once: 'I'm sorry, I had no right to ask you questions about the Professor. I wasn't being nosey, though.'

'I know that, miss, and I ain't one ter gossip, specially about the Professor—'e's a good man, make no mistake, but 'e ain't a 'appy one, neither.' Caro poured a cup of coffee and waited. 'It used ter be an 'ouse full when I first come 'ere. Eighteen years ago, it were—come over on 'oliday, I did, and took a fancy ter living 'ere after I met Marta. She was already working 'ere, kitchenmaid then, that was when the Professor's ma and pa were alive. Died in a car accident, they did, and he ups and marries a couple of years after that. Gay times they were, when the young Baroness was 'ere…'

'Baroness?'

Noakes scratched his head. 'Well, miss, the Professor's a baron as well as a professor, if yer take my meaning.'

'How long ago did he marry, Noakes?' Caroline was so afraid that he would stop telling her the rest, and she did want to know.

'It was in 1966, miss, two years after his folk died. Pretty lady she was, too, very gay, 'ated 'im being a doctor, always working, she used ter say, and when 'e was 'ome, looking after the estate. She liked a gay life, I can tell you! She left 'im, miss, two years after they were married—ran away with some man or other and they both got killed in a plane crash a few months later.'

Caro had let her coffee get cold. So that was why

the Professor shunned her company—he must have loved his wife very dearly. She said quietly: 'Thank you for telling me, Noakes. I'm glad he's got you and Mrs Noakes and Juffrouw Kropp to look after him.'

'That we do, miss. Shall I warm up that coffee? It must be cold.'

'It's lovely, thank you. I think I'll have a nap before lunch.'

But she didn't go to sleep, she didn't even doze. She sat thinking of the Professor; he had asked her if she were lonely, but it was he who was the truly lonely one.

CHAPTER TWO

THE PROFESSOR TOOK the stitches out of Caro's leg the next morning and his manner towards her was such as to discourage her from showing any of the sympathy she felt for him. He had wished her a chilly good morning, assured her that she would feel no pain, and proceeded about his business without more ado. Then he had stood back and surveyed the limb, pronounced it healing nicely, applied a pad and bandage and suggested that she might like to go downstairs.

'Well, yes, I should, very much,' said Caro, and smiled at him, to receive an icy stare in return which sent the colour to her cheeks. But she wasn't easily put off. 'May I wear my clothes?' she asked him. 'This dressing gown's borrowed from someone and I expect they'd like it back. Besides, I'm sick of it.'

His eyebrows rose. 'It was lent in kindness,' he pointed out.

She stammered a little. 'I didn't mean that—you must think I'm ungrateful, but I'm not—what I meant was it's a bit big for me and I'd like…'

He had turned away. 'You have no need to explain yourself, Miss Tripp. I advise you not to do too much today. The wound on your leg was deep and is not yet soundly healed.' He had left her, feeling that she had made a mess of things again. And she had no sympathy for him at all, she assured herself; let him moulder into middle age with his books and his papers and his lectures!

With Marta's help she dressed in a sweater and pleated skirt and was just wondering if she was to walk downstairs on her own when Noakes arrived. He held a stout stick in one hand and offered her his arm.

'The Professor says you're to go very slowly and lean on me,' he advised her, 'and take the stairs one at a time.' He smiled at her. 'Like an old lady,' he added.

It took quite a time, but she didn't mind because it gave her time to look around her as they passed from one stair to the next. The hall was even bigger than she had remembered and the room into which she was led quite took her breath away. It was lofty and square and furnished with large comfortable chairs and sofas, its walls lined with cabinets displaying silver and china and in between these, portraits in heavy frames. There was a fire in the enormous hearth and a chair drawn up to it with a small table beside it upon which was a pile of magazines and newspapers.

'The Professor told me ter get something for yer to read, miss,' said Noakes, 'and I done me best. After lunch, if yer feels like it, I'll show yer the library.'

'Oh, Noakes, you're all so kind, and I've given you all such a lot of extra work.'

He looked astonished. 'Lor' luv yer, miss—we enjoy 'aving yer—it's quiet, like yer said.'

'Yes. Noakes, I've heard a dog barking…'

'That'll be Rex, miss. 'E's a quiet beast mostly, but 'e barks when the Professor comes in. Marta's got a little cat too.'

'Oh, has she? So have I—his name's Waterloo, and my landlady's looking after him while I'm away. It'll be nice to see him again.'

'Yes, miss. Juffrouw Kropp'll bring coffee for you.'

It was indeed quiet, sitting there by herself. Caroline leafed through the newspapers and tried to get interested in the news and then turned to the magazines. It was almost lunchtime when she heard the Professor's voice in the hall and she sat up, put a hand to her hair and then put on a cheerful face, just as though she were having the time of her life. But he didn't come into the room. She heard his voice receding and a door shutting and presently Juffrouw Kropp brought in her lunch tray, set it on the table beside her and smilingly went away again. Caro had almost finished the delicious little meal when she heard the Professor's voice again, speaking to Noakes as he crossed the hall and left the house.

She was taken to the library by a careful Noakes after lunch and settled into a chair by one of the circular tables in that vast apartment, but no sooner had he gone than she picked up her stick, eased herself out of her chair and began a tour of the bookshelves which lined the entire room. The books were in several languages and most of them learned ones, but there were a number of novels in English and a great many medical books in that language. But she rejected them all for a Dutch-English dictionary; it had occurred to her that since she was to spend several more days as the Professor's guest, she might employ her time in learning a word or two of his language. She was deep in this task, muttering away to herself when Noakes brought a tea tray, arranged it by her, and asked her if she was quite comfortable.

'Yes, Noakes, thank you—I'm teaching myself some Dutch words. But I don't think I'm pronouncing them properly.'

'I daresay not, miss. Tell yer what, when Juffrouw Kropp comes later, get 'er ter 'elp yer. She's a dab hand at it. Nasty awkward language it is—took me years ter learn.'

'But you always speak English with the Professor?'

'That's right, miss—comes as easy to 'im as his own language!'

Caroline ate her tea, feeling much happier now that she had something to do, and when Juffrouw Kropp came to light the lamps presently, she asked that lady to sit down for a minute and help her.

Caro had made a list of words, and now she tried them out on the housekeeper, mispronouncing them dreadfully, and then, because she was really interested, correcting them under her companion's guidance. It whiled away the early evening until the housekeeper had to go, leaving her with the assurance that Noakes would be along presently to help her back to her room.

But it wasn't Noakes who came in, it was the Professor, walking so quietly that she didn't look up from her work, only said: 'Noakes, Juffrouw Kropp has been such a help, only there's a word here and I can't remember…'

She looked round and stopped, because the Professor was standing quite close by, looking at her. She answered his quiet good evening cheerfully and added: 'So sorry, I expected Noakes, he's coming to help me up to my room. I'd have gone sooner if I'd known you were home.'

She fished the stick up from the floor beside her and stood up, gathering the dictionary and her pen and paper into an awkward bundle under one arm, only to have them removed immediately by the Professor.

He said stiffly: 'Will you dine with me this evening? Since you are already downstairs...'

Caroline was so surprised that she didn't answer at once, and when she did her soft voice was so hesitant that it sounded like a stammer.

'Thank you for asking me, but I won't, thank you.' She put out a hand for the dictionary and he transferred it to the other hand, out of her reach.

'Why not?' He looked annoyed and his voice was cold.

'You don't really want me,' she said frankly. 'You said that I wasn't to—to interfere with your life in any way and I said I wouldn't.' She added kindly: 'I'm very happy, thank you, I've never been so spoiled in all my life.' She held out her hand; this time he gave her the dictionary.

'Just as you wish,' he said with a politeness she found more daunting than coldness. He took the stick from her, then took her arm and helped her out of the room and across the hall. At the bottom of the staircase he picked her up and carried her to the wide gallery above and across it to her room. At the door, he set her down and opened it for her. His 'Goodnight,

Miss Tripp' was quite without expression. Caroline had no way of knowing if he was relieved that she had refused his invitation or if he was angry about it. She gave him a quiet goodnight and went through the door, to undress slowly and get ready for bed; she would have a bath and have her supper in her dressing gown by the fire.

Marta came presently to help her into the bath, turn down the bed and fuss nicely round the room, and after her came one of the maids with her supper; soup and a cheese souffle with a salad on the side and a Bavarian creme to follow. Caroline didn't think the Professor would be eating that, nor would he be drinking the home-made lemonade she was offered.

The house was very quiet when she woke the next morning and when Marta brought her her breakfast tray, she told her that Noakes had gone with the Professor to the airfield just south of the city and would bring the car back later.

'Has the Professor gone away?' asked Caroline, feeling unaccountably upset.

'To England and then to Paris—he has, how do you say? the lecture.'

'How long for?' asked Caro.

Marta shrugged her shoulders. 'I do not know—five, six days, perhaps longer.'

Which meant that when he came home again she would go almost at once—perhaps he wanted that.

She ate her breakfast listlessly and then got herself up and dressed. Her leg was better, it hardly ached at all and neither did her head. She trundled downstairs slowly and went into the library again where she spent a busy morning conning more Dutch words. There didn't seem much point in it, but it was something to do.

After lunch she went into the garden. It was a chilly day with the first bite of autumn in the air and Juffrouw Kropp had fastened her into a thick woollen cape which dropped around her ankles and felt rather heavy. But she was glad of it presently when she had walked a little way through the formal gardens at the side of the house and found a seat under an arch of beech. It afforded a good view of her surroundings and she looked slowly around her. The gardens stretched away on either side of her and she supposed the meadows beyond belonged to the house too, for there was a high hedge beyond them. The house stood, of red brick, mellowed with age, its many windows gleaming in the thin sunshine; it was large with an important entrance at the top of a double flight of steps, but it was very pleasant too. She could imagine it echoing to the shouts of small children and in the winter evenings its windows would glow with light and guests would stream in to spend the evening…not, of course, in reality, she thought sadly; the Professor had turned himself into a kind of hermit, excluding everyone and everything from his life except work and books. 'I must try and make him smile,' she said out loud, and fell to wondering how she might do that.

It was the following morning, while she was talking to Noakes as he arranged the coffee tray beside her in the library, that they fell to discussing Christmas.

'Doesn't the Professor have family or friends to stay?' asked Caro.

'No, miss. Leastways, 'e 'olds an evening party—very grand affair it is too—but 'e ain't got no family, not in this country. Very quiet time it is.'

'No carols?'

Noakes shook his head. 'More's the pity—I like a nice carol, meself.'

Caro poured out her coffee. 'Noakes, why shouldn't you have them this year? There are—how many? six of you altogether, aren't there? Couldn't you teach everyone the words? I mean, they don't have to know what they mean—aren't there any Dutch carols?'

'Plenty, miss, only it ain't easy with no one ter play the piano. We'd sound a bit silly like.'

'I can play. Noakes, would it be a nice idea to learn one or two carols and sing them for the Professor at Christmas—I mean, take him by surprise?'

Noakes looked dubious. Caroline put her cup

down. 'Look, Noakes, everyone loves Christmas—
if you could just take him by surprise, it might make
it seem more fun. Then perhaps he'd have friends to
stay—or something.'

It suddenly seemed very important to her that the
Professor should enjoy his Christmas, and Noakes,
looking at her earnest face, found himself agreeing.
'We could 'ave a bash, miss. There's a piano in the
drawing room and there's one in the servants' sitting-room.'

'Would you mind if I played it? I wouldn't want
to intrude…'

'Lor' luv yer, miss, we'd be honoured.'

She went with him later that day, through the
baize door at the back of the hall, down a flagstoned
passage and through another door into a vast kitchen,
lined with old-fashioned dressers and deep cupboards. Marta was at the kitchen table and Juffrouw
Kropp was sitting in a chair by the Aga, and they
looked up and smiled as she went in. Noakes guided
her to a door at the end and opened it on to a very
comfortably furnished room with a large table at one
end, easy chairs, a TV in a corner and a piano against
one wall. There was a stove halfway along the further wall and warm curtains at the windows. The
Professor certainly saw to it that those who worked
for him were comfortable. Caroline went over to the
piano and opened it, sat down and began to play. She

was by no means an accomplished pianist, but she played with feeling and real pleasure. She forgot Noakes for the moment, tinkling her way through a medley of Schubert, Mozart and Brahms until she was startled to hear him clapping and turned to see them all standing by the door watching her.

'Cor, yer play a treat, miss,' said Noakes. 'I suppose yer don't 'appen to know *Annie Get Yer Gun?*'

She knew some of it; before she had got to the end they were clapping their hands in time to the music and Noakes was singing. When she came to a stop finally, he said: 'Never mind the carols, miss, if yer'd just play now and then—something we could all sing?'

He sounded wistful, and looking round at their faces she saw how eager they were to go on with the impromptu singsong. 'Of course I'll play,' she said at once. 'You can tell me what you want and I'll do my best.' She smiled round at them all; Noakes and Marta and Juffrouw Kropp, the three young maids and someone she hadn't seen before, a quite old man—the gardener, she supposed. 'Shall I play something else?' she asked.

She sat there for an hour and when she went she had promised that she would go back the following evening. And on the way upstairs she asked Noakes if she might look at the piano in the drawing-room.

She stood in the doorway, staring around her. The

piano occupied a low platform built under the window at one end, it was a grand and she longed to play upon it; she longed to explore the room too, its panelled walls hung with portraits, its windows draped with heavy brocade curtains. The hearth had a vast hood above it with what she supposed was a coat of arms carved upon it. All very grand, but it would be like trespassing to go into the room without the Professor inviting her to do so, and she didn't think he would be likely to do that. She thanked a rather mystified Noakes and went on up to her room.

Lying in bed later, she thought how nice it would be to explore the house. She had had glimpses of it, but there were any number of closed doors she could never hope to have opened for her. Still, she reminded herself bracingly, she was being given the opportunity of staying in a lovely old house and being waited on hand and foot. Much later she heard Noakes locking up and Rex barking. She hadn't met him yet; Noakes had told her that he was to be kept out of her way until she was quite secure on her feet. 'Mild as milk,' he had said, 'but a bit on the big side.' Caroline had forgotten to ask what kind of dog he was. Tomorrow she would contrive to meet him; her leg was rapidly improving, indeed it hardly hurt at all, only when she was tired.

Her thoughts wandered on the verge of sleep. Would the Professor expect to be reimbursed for his

trouble and his professional services, she wondered,
and if so how would one set about it? Perhaps the
hospital would settle with him if and when he sent a
bill. He wouldn't be bothered to do that himself, she
decided hazily; she had seen a serious middle-aged
woman only that morning as she crossed the hall on
her way to the library and Noakes had told her that
it was the secretary, Mevrouw Slikker, who came
daily to attend to the Professor's correspondence.
Undoubtedly she would be businesslike about it.
Caro nodded her sleepy head at this satisfactory so-
lution and went to sleep.

  She walked a little further the next day, following
the paths around the gardens and sitting down now
and again to admire her surroundings. She wondered
if the Professor ever had the time to admire his own
grounds and thought probably not, he was certainly
never long enough in his own house to enjoy its com-
forts and magnificence. She wandered round to the
back of the house and found a pleasing group of old
buildings grouped round a courtyard, barns and stables and a garage and a shed which smelled deliciously of apples and corn. It was coming out of this
interesting place that she came face to face with an
Old English sheepdog. He stood almost to her waist
and peered at her with a heavily eyebrowed whiskered face. 'Rex!' she cried. 'Oh, aren't you a darling!' She extended a closed fist and he sniffed at it

and then put an enormous paw on each of her shoulders and reared up to peer down at her. He must have liked what he saw, for he licked her face gently, got down on to his four feet again and offered a head for scratching. They finished their walk together and wandered in through a little side door to find Noakes looking anxious.

'There you are, miss—I 'opes yer 'aven't been too far.' His elderly eyes fell upon Rex. ''E didn't frighten yer? 'E's always in the kitchen with Marta in the mornings. I'll take 'im back…'

'Oh, Noakes, please could he stay with me? He's company and ever so gentle. Is he allowed in the house?'

'Lor' yes, miss. Follows the Professor round like a shadow, 'e does. Well, I don't see no 'arm.' He beamed at her. 'There's a nice lunch for yer in the library and Juffrouw Kropp says if yer wants 'er this afternoon she's at yer disposal.'

So the day passed pleasantly enough, and the following two days were just as pleasant. Caro did a little more each day now; the Professor would be back in two days' time, Noakes had told her, and she had to be ready to leave then. She had no intention of trespassing on his kindness for an hour longer than she needed to. Of course she would have to get tickets for the journey home, but that shouldn't take long, and Noakes would help her and perhaps the

Professor would allow him to drive her to the station in Leeuwarden; she had already discovered that the train went all the way to the Hoek—all she would need to do was to get from it to the boat. She had mentioned it carefully to Noakes when he had been clearing away her supper dishes, but he had shaken his head and said dubiously that it would be better to consult the Professor. ''E may not want yer to go straight away, miss,' he suggested.

'Well, I should think he would,' she told him matter-of-factly, 'for I'm quite well now and after all, he didn't invite me as a guest. He's been more than kind to let me get well here and I mustn't stay longer than absolutely necessary.'

Noakes had shaken his head and muttered to himself and then begged her to go down to the sitting-room and play for them all again—something she had done with great pleasure, for it passed the evenings very nicely. When she was on her own she found that she had an increasing tendency to think about the Professor—a pointless pastime, she told herself, and went on doing it nonetheless.

It rained the next day, so that she spent a great deal of it in the library, with Rex beside her, poring over her dictionary. She was making progress, or so she thought, with an ever-lengthening list of words which she tried out on members of the staff. All rather a waste of time, she knew that, but it passed the days and in some obscure way made the Professor a little less of a stranger. She went earlier than usual to play the piano that day, perhaps because the afternoon was unnaturally dark and perhaps because she was lonely despite Rex's company. And Noakes and his staff seemed pleased to see her, requesting this, that and the other tune, beating time and tra-la-ing away to each other. Presently, with everyone satisfied, Caroline began to play to please herself; half forgotten melodies she had enjoyed before her aunt had married again and then on to Sibelius and Grieg, not noticing how quiet everyone had become; she was halfway through a wistful little French tune when she stopped and turned round. 'Sorry, I got carried away,' she began, and saw the Professor standing in the doorway, his hands in his pockets, leaning against the door frame.

He didn't smile, indeed, he was looking coldly furious, although his icily polite: 'Pray don't stop on my account, Miss Tripp,' was uttered in a quiet voice.

Caroline stood up rather too hard on the bad leg so that she winced. 'You're angry,' she said quickly, 'and I'm sorry—I have no right to be here, but you're not to blame Noakes or anyone else—I invited myself.'

She wanted to say a great deal more, but the look of annoyance on his face stopped her. She wished everyone goodnight in her newly acquired Dutch and went past him through the door and along the passage. He caught up with her quite easily before she could reach the staircase, and she sighed soundlessly. He was going to lecture her and she might as well have it now as later; perhaps she might even get him to see that no harm had been done, indeed he might even be glad that his staff had enjoyed a pleasant hour.

She turned to face him. 'It's a pity you frown so,' she said kindly.

He looked down his splendid nose at her. 'I have very good reason to frown, Miss Tripp, and well you know it. I return home unexpectedly and what do I find? My butler, my housekeeper, my cook, the maidservants and the gardener being entertained by you in the servants' sitting-room. Probably if I had come home even earlier I should have found you all playing gin rummy in the cellars.'

She made haste to reassure him. 'Not gin rummy—it was canasta, and we played round the kitchen table—just for half an hour,' she added helpfully. 'You see, I'm learning Dutch.'

His fine mouth curved into a sneer. 'Indeed? I cannot think why.'

Caroline said in her quiet hesitant voice: 'Well, it's something to do, you know. I'm quite well, you see.'

His voice was silky and his voice cold. 'Miss

Tripp, you have disrupted my household—when one considers that I have done my best to help you and I find your behaviour intolerable.'

She stared back at him, her lip caught between her teeth, because it was beginning to tremble. After a long moment she said: 'I'm sorry, Professor.'

He turned on his heel. 'I'm glad to hear it—I hope you will mend your ways.'

He went into his study without another word and she went to her room, where she sat on her bed to review the situation. The Professor was going out to dinner that evening, she had heard Noakes say so—to one of his grand friends, she supposed, where the girls knew better than to play the piano in the servants' room and said things to make him smile instead of frown. Oh well…she got up and went across to the tallboy where her few possessions were housed and laid them on the bed, fetched her duffle bag from the cupboard and began to pack. She did it neatly and unhurriedly. There was plenty of time; she would eat her supper alone presently, as she always did, and when everyone had gone to the kitchen for their own meal, she would slip away. She would have to leave a letter. She frowned a long while over its composition, but at length it was done, neatly written and sealed into an envelope. She would have to leave it somewhere where Noakes wouldn't find it at once. The Professor's study would be the best place, he always went straight there when he came home, shutting himself away in his own learned lonely world—for he was lonely, Caroline was sure of that.

She finished her packing and went down to her supper which this evening had been set in the dining room, a richly sombre place. She felt quite lost sitting at the great oval table surrounded by all the massive furniture, but she made a good meal, partly to please Noakes and partly because she wasn't sure when she would have the next one. And Noakes was uneasy, although the Professor, he assured her, hadn't been in the least angry—indeed, he had hardly mentioned the matter. Noakes hoped—they all hoped—that tomorrow she would play for them again, but first he would ascertain if the Professor objected to her visiting the servants' sitting-room.

Caroline made some cheerful reply, finished her meal, mentioned that she would go to bed early and went upstairs. When she crept down half an hour later there was no sound. Everyone was in the kitchens by now and she wouldn't be missed, probably not until the morning, or at least until the Professor came home, and that would be late. She had put on her anorak, counted her money carefully and carried her bag downstairs before going to the study and putting the letter on the Professor's desk. She paused in the doorway for a last look; his desk was an orderly clutter of papers and books and his chair was pushed to one side as though he had got up in a hurry. She sighed deeply, closed the door gently, picked up the duffle bag and went to the door. Her leg was aching a little and she had bandaged it firmly because as far as she knew she would have to walk quite a distance before she could get a bus—the nearest village wasn't too far away, she had found that out from Juffrouw Kropp. If there wasn't a bus she would have to thumb a lift.

She put out a reluctant hand and opened the door. It was heavy, but it swung back on well-oiled hinges, revealing the Professor, key in hand, about to open it from outside. Caro, taken completely by surprise, stood with her mouth open, gaping at him. He, on the other hand, evinced no surprise, nor did he speak, merely took her duffle bag from her, put a large hand on her chest and pushed her very gently back into the house, and then just as gently shut the door behind him. Only then did he ask: 'And where were you going, Caroline?'

'Home—well, the hospital, actually.' He had never called her Caroline before—no one called her that, but it sounded rather nice.

'Why?' He stood blocking her path, the duffle bag on the floor beside him.

It seemed silly to have to explain something to him which he already knew all about. 'I've upset your household: I can quite see that I've been a perfect nuisance to you. I'm very grateful for all you've done for me—and your kindness—but I'm quite able to go back now and… Well, thank you again.'

His harsh laugh made her jump. Quite forgetting to be meek, she said severely: 'And there's no need to laugh when someone thanks you!'

'It strikes me as ironic that you should express gratitude for something you haven't had. I cannot remember being kind to you—I merely did what any other person would have done in similar circumstances, and with the minimum of trouble to myself. If I had been a poor man with a wife and children to care for and had offered you help and shelter at the cost of my and their comfort, that would have been quite a different kettle of fish. As it is, I must confess that I have frequently forgotten that you were in the house.'

Caro didn't speak. A kind of despair had rendered her dumb; her head was full of a mixed bag of thoughts, most of them miserable.

He put out a hand and touched her cheek awkwardly. 'Have you been lonely?'

Living in a bedsitter had taught her not to be lonely. She shook her head, still feeling the touch of his finger.

'And you will be glad to get back—to your flat and your friends. I doubt if you will be allowed to work for a little while.'

She had found her voice at last. It came out in a defiant mutter: 'I shall be awfully glad to get back.'

The gentleness had gone out of his voice; it sounded cold and distant again, just as though he didn't care what she did. 'Yes—I see. But be good enough to wait until the morning. I will arrange a passage for you on the night ferry tomorrow and Noakes shall drive you to the Hoek and see you on board.'

Caroline said stiffly: 'Thank you.'

'You have sufficient money?'

She nodded dumbly.

'Then go to bed.' His eye had caught her bandaged leg. 'Your leg is worse?'

'No. I—I put a crepe bandage on it because I thought I might have to walk for a bit.'

He stared at her without expression, then: 'Come to the study and I will take a look and if necessary rebandage it.'

He prodded and poked with gentle fingers, dressed it lightly and said: 'That should see you safely to Oliver's—get it looked at as soon as you can. It will do better without a dressing.' He held the study door open and offered a hand. 'Goodbye, Caroline.'

His hand was cool and firm and she didn't want to let it go.

'Goodbye, Professor. I shall always be grateful to

you—and I'm sorry that I—I disturbed your peace and quiet.'

Just for a moment she thought he was going to say something, but he didn't.

CHAPTER THREE

CARO ARRIVED BACK at Meadow Road during the morning and the moment she opened the door of number twenty-six, Mrs Hodge bounced out of her basement flat, avid for a good gossip.

'Your friends came,' she said without preamble, 'said you had a bad cut leg and concussion; nasty thing concussion; you could 'ave died.' She eyed Caro's leg with relish and then looked disappointed, and Caro said almost apologetically:

'I don't need a bandage any more. Thank you for looking after Waterloo, Mrs Hodge.'

'No trouble.' Mrs Hodge, a woman who throve on other people's troubles, felt her sympathy had been wasted. 'Your rent's due on Monday.'

Caro edged past her with the duffle bag. 'Yes, I know, Mrs Hodge. I'll just see to Waterloo and unpack and then go back to the hospital and see when I'm to go back.'

She went up the stairs and unlocked the door at the back of the landing. Not one of Mrs Hodge's best rooms, but it was quieter because it overlooked back yards and there was a tiny balcony which was nice for Waterloo.

He came to meet her now and she picked him up and laid him on her shoulder while he purred in her ear, delighted to have her back. Caroline sat down on the divan which did duty as a bed at night and looked around her.

The room was small and rather dark and seemed even more so after the Professor's spacious home; she had done the best she could with pretty curtains and cushions and a patchwork cover for the divan, but nothing could quite disguise the cheap furniture or the sink in one corner with the tiny gas cooker beside it. Caro, not given to being sorry for herself, felt a lump in her throat; it was all such a cruel contrast... She missed them all, the Professor, even though he didn't like her, Noakes and Marta, Juffrouw Kropp... She had been utterly spoilt, waited on hand and foot, and she, who had never been spoilt, had loved it. Right up until the moment she had gone on board, too, with Noakes seeing to her bag and getting her magazines to read and having a word with someone or other so that she had a super cabin to herself and a delicious meal before she had gone to bed. She had tried to pay him, but he had said very firmly that the Professor would deal with that later. Caroline had hoped that although he had said goodbye to her, she would have seen the Professor again before she left, but he had left the house after breakfast and wasn't back when she went away, with the entire staff gathered at the door to see her off.

She roused herself, gave Waterloo a saucer of milk and put on the kettle; a cup of tea would cheer her up and when she had drunk it she would unpack, dust and tidy her room and go round to Oliver's, and on the way back she would buy a few flowers to brighten up the place.

In the office at Oliver's, standing in front of Miss Veron's desk, she was astonished to hear from that lady that the Professor had written a letter about her, suggesting in the politest manner possible that she should have a few days' sick leave before she resumed work on the wards.

'A good idea, Staff Nurse,' said Miss Veron kindly. 'I expect you would like to go home or visit friends—suppose you report for duty in five days' time? You'll go back to Women's Surgical, of course. I'm sure Sister will be glad to see you.'

Caro thanked her and walked slowly back through the busy streets to Meadow Road, stopping on the way to do some shopping and indulge in the extravagance of a bunch of flowers. She would have been glad to have gone straight back to work, for she had no family and although she had a number of friends, to invite herself to go and stay with them was something she had never even dreamed of. So she spent the next four days giving her room an extra clean, reading the books she fetched from the library and talking to Waterloo. She hadn't let anyone at the hospital know that she was back; they would have been round like a flash with offers to go to the cinema, invitations to go out to a meal—morning coffee. But most of them had boyfriends or family and she shrank from being pitied; only a few of her closest friends knew that she had no family and that she hated to talk about it. Actually she need not have worried about being pitied, for she turned a bright face to the world; those who didn't know her well considered her a self-sufficient girl bent on a career, and her close friends took care never to mention it.

She went back on duty on the fifth morning, but she didn't see her friends until the coffee break when they all met in the canteen. The precious fifteen minutes was spent in answering questions; Clare, Stacey and Miriam were all there, wanting to know how she had got on, whether her leg was quite better, whether she had enjoyed herself, whether the Professor had entertained her…

'Well, not to say entertain,' observed Caro. 'He was very kind to me and saw to my leg and took me to be X-rayed at the hospital in Leeuwarden. I—I kept out of his way as much as I could—I mean, he is an important man, Noakes says, and had very little leisure.'

'I could go for him,' said Stacey. 'A bit old, perhaps, but very elegant and a man of the world, if you know what I mean, if only he'd come out from his books and lectures. He must have been crossed in love!'

Caro didn't say anything. She wasn't going to tell them about his wife; it was all a long time ago and besides, it had been a confidence on Noakes' part. She shuddered, imagining the Professor's cold rage if he ever discovered that she knew about his past unhappiness, and Miriam, noticing it, asked: 'What's worrying you, Caro? Is the ward busy?'

Caro was glad to change the subject and talked about something which lasted them until it was time to return to their wards.

Women's Surgical was busy all right; what with Sir Eustace Jenkins' round, a twice-weekly event which was stage-managed as carefully as any royal procession; yesterday's operations cases still attached to drips and tubes and underwater pumps and needing constant care and attention, and over and above these, the normal ward routine of dressings and escorting to X-Ray, Physiotherapy and the usual thundering round looking for notes and Path. Lab. forms which somehow always got mislaid on round days. Caro, hovering at Sister's elbow, ready to interpret that lady's raised eyebrow, shake of the head, or lifted finger and smooth her path to the best of her ability, was quite glad when it was dinner time. She left Sister to serve the puddings and went down to the first meal, queuing for her portion of steamed cod, mashed potato, and butter beans, and devouring it with the rest of her friends at speed so that there would be time to go over to the home and make a pot of tea.

She had more tea presently in Sister's office, having been bidden there to be told that Sister would be going on holiday in a week's time and Caro would be taking over the ward. 'Just for two weeks,' Sister Pringle smiled a little. 'Good practice for you, Caro—you're in the running for my job. I'm leaving to get married in a few months' time and they're keen to get someone who's likely to stay for a few years. After all, I've been here for eight years—they wanted me to stay on, but I've had enough of being a career girl. I'll make way for you.'

Caro, not sure if this was a compliment or an admission that she was unlikely to get married, thanked her superior nicely and hoped that she would be adequate while left in charge.

'Well, I can't see why not—Sir Eustace likes you and you have a nice way with the student nurses.

There are some heavy cases coming in, though, and it'll be take-in week...'

Caro bowed her head obediently over the notes Sister had before her. She wouldn't mind being busy, if she kept her thoughts occupied sufficiently she didn't have time to think about the Professor—a bad habit she had got into, and one which she must conquer even if only for her own peace of mind.

But she continued to think about him a great deal, picturing him alone in that great house, leading a hermit's life. It was a pity, she told Waterloo that evening as she cooked their supper, that he couldn't find some beautiful girl, exactly suited to him, and fall in love with her and get married. No sooner had she thought that than she left the sausages in the pan to fry themselves to a crisp because following hard on its heels was the second thought—that there was nothing in the world she would like more than to be that girl. Only she wasn't beautiful and she certainly wasn't suited to him; she had annoyed him excessively and he must have been delighted to see the back of her.

She sat down on the divan with Waterloo tucked under one arm. On the other hand, if she were given the chance, she would make him happy because that, she knew all at once, was what she wanted to do more than anything else in the world. She gave a watery chuckle. A more ill-suited pair than herself and the Professor would be hard to find, and why, oh, why had she fallen in love with him? Why couldn't it have been someone she might have stood a faint chance of attracting: someone insignificant and uninteresting and used to living on not much money, just sufficiently ambitious to wish to buy his own semi-detached in a suburb and keep his job, recognising in her a kindred spirit.

Only she wasn't a kindred spirit. She hated her narrow life, she wanted to be free; she wasn't sure what she wanted to do, but certainly it wasn't to be tied to a man who didn't look higher than a safe job.

She went on sitting there, oblivious of the sausages and Waterloo's voice reminding her about his supper, lost in a happy daydream where she was beautiful, well dressed and the apple of the Professor's eye. A changed Professor, of course, enjoying the pleasure of life as well as his work, discussing his day with her, planning it so that he could see as much of her as possible—wanting to be with her every minute of his leisure. She would play to him on that beautiful piano in his grand drawing-room, in a pink organza dress, and when he came into his house each evening she would meet him in the hall with their beautiful children around her. It was all absurd and impossible and very real in her mind's eye: if it hadn't been for the smell of burning sausages it might have gone on for hours. As it was, she came back to reality, removed the charred bits from the pan, opened a can of beans, fed Waterloo and made tea before going round to the local library to change her books. She came back with Fodor's Guide to the Netherlands and then spent the evening reading about Friesland, with the Professor's handsome severe features superimposed on every page.

Sister departed a week later, thankfully handing over the ward keys to Caroline with the heartfelt wish that she would be able to manage. 'Not that you're not capable,' said Sister, 'but it's take-in tomorrow.' She added happily: 'We shall be on Majorca—and in swimsuits—can you imagine it? In November, too.'

But there was no time to be envious of Sister Pringle. Take-in weeks were always busy, and this particular one was worse than usual. Several young women were admitted with black eyes, broken noses, cracked bones and severe contusions after taking part in a demonstration march about something or other and falling foul of a rival faction on the way. These had been followed by two victims of a gas explosion in one of the small terraced houses close to the hospital, and no sooner were they settled in their beds than an old lady who had fallen over in the street and cut her head was admitted for observation. Caro found her hands full and they remained like that for most of the week. She sighed with relief when she went off duty on the seventh day. After midnight they would have comparative peace on the ward; she would catch up with the paperwork, see to the off-duty and have time to chat to each of the patients as she took round the post—and the nurses should be able to catch up on their off-duty. She rose from her bed at the beginning of the second week of Sister's absence in the pleasant expectation of an uneventful week.

And so it was for the first few hours. The nurses, happy in the knowledge that there would be no urgent call to ready a bed for yet another emergency, began on the morning's routine with a good will and Caro, having fulfilled her ambition to have a nice long chat with each patient in turn, organised the day's tasks, made a sortie to the X-ray department with the firm determination to discover the whereabouts of a number of missing films, and answered the telephone at least a dozen times, before she settled herself in the office to puzzle out the off-duty for the following two weeks. She was halfway through this tedious task when there was a knock on the door and before she could say anything, it was opened and Professor Thoe van Erckelens stalked in.

Caroline didn't speak, she was too surprised— and besides, after the first second or two, her heart raced so violently that she had no breath. She just sat where she was and stared at him with huge hazel eyes.

'Ha,' observed the Professor, 'you are surprised to see me.'

He looked ill-tempered, tired too. It was an awful waste of one's life to love a man who didn't care a row of pins for one. She took a steadying breath and said in her quiet voice: 'Yes, Professor, I am. I expect you have a consultation here? Shall I...?'

He came right into the office and shut the door. 'No, I came to see you.'

She opened her eyes and her mouth too. 'Whatever for?' She went on earnestly: 'I can't really spare the time unless you wanted to see a patient—there's Mrs Possett's dressing and two patients to go for X-ray.'

He dismissed Mrs Possett with a wave of his hand. 'What I have to say will take five minutes—less.'

Caroline folded her small, nicely cared for hands in her lap and gave him her full attention. He didn't move from the door. 'Will you marry me, Caroline?'

She stayed very still. After a moment she asked: 'Me? Is this a joke or something, Professor?'

'No, and if you will be good enough to give me your full attention and not interrupt I will explain.'

She glanced around her just to make sure that she wasn't dreaming. The office was much as usual, its desk an orderly muddle of forms and charts and papers, chilly, foggy air coming in through the open window, the radiator as usual gurgling gently into tepid warmth. The only difference was the Professor, taking up most of the available space and apparently suffering from a brainstorm. She said in a tranquil voice which quite masked her bewilderment: 'I'm listening,' and made herself look at him. She was rewarded by a forbidding stare.

'I'm forty,' he told her almost angrily. 'I have been married before—thirteen years ago, to be precise. My wife left me for another man within two years of our marriage and she—both of them—were killed in an accident a year later. I have had no wish to marry again.' He shrugged huge shoulders, 'Why should I? I have my work, enough money, a well run home and there are always girls—pretty girls if I should wish for female company.'

He paused to study her and she flinched because no doubt he was comparing her homely face with the young ladies in question. 'However, after you had left my house I missed you—my household miss you. They have worn gloomy faces ever since you left—quite ridiculous, of course—even Rex and the cats...' He paused again, searching her quiet face as though he were trying to discover what there was about her that could disrupt his organised life. Presently he went on. 'You are an extraordinary girl,' he declared irritably, 'you have no looks, no witty conversation, quite deplorable clothes—and yet I find that I am able to talk to you—indeed, I find myself wishing to discuss the various happenings of my day with you. I am not in love with you and I have no wish to be; I need a calm quiet companion, someone sensible who isn't for ever wanting to be taken out to dinner or the theatre, nor demand to know where I am going each time I leave the house. I need... I need...'

'A sheet anchor,' supplied Caro in a sensible voice. 'No demands, no curiosity, just a—someone to talk to when you feel inclined.'

He looked surprised. 'You understand then; I have no need to explain myself further. And above all, no romantic nonsense!' He gave her a bleak look which wrung her soft heart. 'You will have a pleasant life; the servants are already devoted to you and you will have my friends and sufficient money. And in return I ask for companionship when I need it, someone to sit at my table and play hostess to my guests and run my home as I like it. Well?'

Caro studied his face. He meant every preposterous word of it and he expected her to say yes then and there. I must change him just a little, she thought lovingly, he must be got out of his lonely arrogant world and learn to enjoy himself again—he must have been happy once. Aloud she said in a tranquil voice: 'I must have time to think about it.'

'Time? Why should you need time? You have no family.' He looked deliberately round the little room. 'And nothing but a hard-working future.'

Here was another one who took it for granted that no one wanted to marry her. 'You make it sound like a bribe,' she told him.

His mouth was a straight bad-tempered line. 'Nothing of the sort. I have offered you marriage. I hope that I am not such a hypocrite that I pretend affection for you—liking, yes; you annoy me excessively at times and yet I must admit that I like you. Well?'

She smiled a little. 'I'll tell you tomorrow. I must sleep on it.'

'Oh, very well, if you want it that way. I thought you were a sensible girl.'

'I am, that's why I have to think about it.'

There was a knock on the door and he opened it, glaring at the student nurse standing outside so that she sidled past him uneasily.

'It's all right, Nurse,' said Caro soothingly. 'What's the matter?'

'Mrs Skipton's dressing's down ready for you to see, Staff.'

'I'm coming now,' she smiled reassuringly, and the nurse retreated, casting an interested eye upon the Professor as she went—a remarkably handsome man even though he looked as black as a thundercloud.

He closed the door with a snap behind her and then stood in front of it so that although Caro had got to her feet she was forced to a halt before him. 'I do have to go,' she told him mildly.

He opened the door. 'I'll see you tomorrow, Caroline.'

She walked past him into the ward, looking as serene as she always did while her insides turned somersaults. The nurse who had been to the office rolled her eyes upwards and shrugged her shoulders for the benefit of the junior nurse with her. 'Poor old Staff,' she murmured, 'as prim as a maiden aunt even with that gorgeous man actually talking to her!'

'I'll have the forceps, Nurse,' said Caro briskly. She had seen the look and rightly guessed at the murmur. It would be fun, she mused as she deftly removed the rubber drain from Mrs Skipton's shrinking person, to see the girl's face when she announced her engagement to the Professor.

Because she was going to marry him, she had no doubts about that, and not for any of the reasons he had given her, either. He hadn't even thought of the only reason which mattered—that she loved him.

It was typical of the Professor not to mention when and where he would see her on the following day. Caroline spent the whole of it in a state of pleasurable excitement, one ear cocked for the telephone, and her eyes sliding to the ward door every time it opened. In the end she went off duty after tea, telling herself that he had forgotten all about her, thought better of it, or what seemed more likely, she had dreamed the whole thing. She explained this to

Waterloo at some length as she gave him his supper and then went to peer into the cupboard and see what she could cook for her own meal. A tin of soup, she decided, and then a poached egg on toast with a pot of tea. And while she had it she would finish that interesting bit in Fodor's Guide about Friesland having its own national anthem. She knelt to light the gas fire, but before she could strike a match there was a knock on the door. Her heart shot into her mouth, but she ignored it; the Professor had no idea where she lived and she hoped and prayed that he never would. It would be her landlady, she supposed, and went to open the door.

She had supposed wrong. It was the Professor, looming large on the narrow landing. The sheer size of him forced her to retreat a few steps so that he was inside before she could say a word. He stood looking around him unhurriedly and asked: 'This is your flat?'

'Good evening,' said Caro, and didn't answer him.

He turned his eyes on to her then. 'I've annoyed you—probably you didn't wish me to know that you lived in a bedsitter in this truly deplorable neighbourhood.'

'It's convenient for Oliver's.' She added indignantly: 'It's my home.'

His eyes lighted on Waterloo, waiting impatiently for the fire to be lighted. 'Your cat?'

'Yes—Waterloo. I found him there when he was a kitten.'

'He will of course return with us to Huis Thoe.'

She had scrambled to her feet. 'But I haven't said I'd…marry you.'

'Perhaps we might go somewhere and have dinner and discuss it.'

She stared at him, wondering if there was another girl in the world who had had such a dry-as-dust proposal. Her first inclination was to refuse, but she was hungry and soup and an egg weren't exactly gastronomic excitements. 'I'll have to change,' she said.

'I will wait on the landing.' He opened the door and a strong aroma of frying onions caused his winged nostrils to flare. He didn't speak, only gave her an eloquent look as he closed it quietly.

There wasn't much choice in the rickety wardrobe, but the few clothes she had were presentable although the Professor had called them deplorable. How would he know anyway, leading the life he did? Caroline put on a plain wool dress of dark green, combed her hair, did things to her face, found her good wool coat, her best shoes, her only decent handbag, gave Waterloo a saucer of food and assured him that she wouldn't be long, and left the room. The Professor was standing quietly, but giving the impression of an impatient man holding his impatience in check with a great effort, and she could hardly blame him; the smell of onions had got considerably worse.

They went down the narrow stairs and out into the street where he took her by the arm and hurried her on to the opposite pavement. 'The car is at Oliver's,' and at her quick questioning glance, 'and if you are wondering why I didn't go and fetch it while you were changing I will admit to a fear that if I did so you might have changed your mind and disappeared by the time I had got back.'

Caroline paused to stare up at him in the dusk. 'Well, really—is that your opinion of me? I would never dream of…'

'I am aware of that; it was merely a remarkably silly notion which entered my head.'

He wasn't going to say any more than that. They walked the short distance in silence and he opened the door of the Aston Martin for her. Settling himself beside her, he remarked: 'I've booked a table at the Savoy Grill Room.'

'Oh, no!' exclaimed Caro involuntarily. 'I'm not dressed…'

'The Grill Room,' he reminded her, and glanced sideways at her. 'You look all right to me.'

She had the idea that he hadn't the vaguest notion of what she was wearing; probably he never would have, for he never really looked at her for more than a few seconds at a time. If it came to that, very few did.

The Grill Room was full and she felt shy of her surroundings as they went in, but they were shown at once to their table and although she would have preferred one in a quiet corner where she could have been quite unnoticed, nothing could have bettered the attention they received.

She sipped at the sherry she had been given and studied the menu, mouthwateringly lengthy; she settled for salmon mousse, tournedos, sautéed straw potatoes and braised celery, and when it came ate it with appetite, replying politely to her companion's desultory conversation as he demolished a grilled steak. She enjoyed the Beaujolais he offered her too, but prudently refused a second glass, which was just as well, for the sherry trifle was deliciously rich. It was when the waiter had cleared the table and set coffee before them that the Professor abandoned his dinner table conversation and asked abruptly: 'Well, you've slept on it, Caroline, and now I should like your answer. Is it yes or no?'

She handed him his coffee cup without haste. He had asked a plain question, he was going to get a plain answer. 'Yes.'

She watched his face as she spoke and found it rather daunting to see his calm expression quite unchanged. 'Very well, we can now make plans for our marriage. As soon as possible, don't you think?'

'Very well, but I have to give in my resignation at Oliver's, Prof… What am I to call you?'

He smiled a little. 'Radinck. If you have no objection, I can arrange that you leave very shortly. We can be married here by special licence. Do you wish to invite anyone? Family? Friends?'

'I have an aunt—no one else—she's married now and I don't think she will want to come to the wedding. I expect some of my friends from the hospital would like to come to the church.'

'I'll see about it and let you know. Have you sufficient money to buy yourself some clothes?'

Caroline thought of her little nest egg, hoarded against a rainy day. 'Yes, thank you.'

He nodded. 'You can of course buy anything you want when we return, but I presume you will want something for the wedding.' His voice held a faint sneer.

'I won't disgrace you,' she told him quietly, and was pleased to see him look a little taken aback. If she hadn't loved him so much she would have been furious.

He begged her pardon stiffly and she said kindly: 'Oh, that's all right—it'll be super to have some decent clothes.' She wrinkled her forehead in thought. 'Something I can travel in and wear afterwards…'

He passed his cup for more coffee. 'Perhaps I should point out to you that you can buy all the clothes you want when you are my wife. I—we shall live comfortably enough.' He sat back in his chair. 'Now as to the actual wedding…'

He had thought of everything; the arrangements for her to leave, the obtaining of the marriage licence, giving up her bedsitter, a basket for Waterloo's comfortable transport to Holland. There would be no honeymoon, he told her, and that didn't surprise her at all, honeymoons were for two people in love, but she was surprised when he said: 'We will go tomorrow and buy the wedding rings and I will give you your engagement ring—I brought it over with me but forgot to bring it with me this evening.'

She didn't know whether to laugh or cry at that.

Radinck took her back to Meadow Road presently, waiting at her front door while she climbed the stairs and unlocked her own door. His goodnight had been casual and, to her ear, faintly impatient. Probably he found her boring company, but in that case why did he want to marry her? Probably he was tired. She got ready for bed, made a pot of tea because she was too excited to sleep and sat in front of the gas fire with Waterloo beside her, politely listening while she recounted the evening's happenings to him.

She was off in the evening again the next day and she supposed Radinck would meet her then; certainly there was no time to go buying wedding rings during the day—but apparently he thought differently.

Caroline had got well into the morning's routine when he came on to the ward with Sir Eustace, and Caro, hastily pulling down her sleeves, went down the ward to meet them, wondering which patient they wanted to see.

They wished her good morning and Sir Eustace said jovially: 'Well, Staff Nurse, I am delighted at the news that you are to marry. I haven't come to do a round, only to beg the pleasure of giving you away.'

Caro pinkened. 'Oh, would you? Would you really? I did wonder... I haven't got any relations...'

'I shall be delighted—Radinck will let me know the day when you've decided it.' He beamed at her. 'And now I must go to theatre—I'm already late.'

She escorted him to the door and went back to the Professor, who hadn't said a word after his good morning and in answer to her look of enquiry he observed: 'It is rather public here, perhaps we might go to the office for a minute.'

She led the way, offered him a seat which he declined and sat down at the desk. 'I will be outside at twelve o'clock,' he told her. 'You will go to your dinner then, I believe? We can go along to Apsleys and get the rings and have a quick lunch somewhere.'

'But I'll be in uniform—there's only an hour, you

know—there'll never be time… I don't mind missing lunch.'

'Put a coat over your uniform. I'll see that you get back on duty on time.' He took a small box out of a pocket. 'This was my mother's—she had small hands, like yours, and I hope it will fit.'

He opened the box and took out a great sapphire ring set in a circle of rose diamonds and when she held out her hand, slipped it on to her finger. It fitted exactly. Caro, who was inclined to be superstitious, thought it was a good omen.

She thanked him for it and longed to throw her arms round him and kiss him, but instead she said: 'It's very beautiful: I'll take great care of it.'

He nodded carelessly. 'You will wish to get on with your work—I'll meet you at noon.'

He had gone before she could do more than nod.

It wasn't entirely satisfactory going out in her winter coat which was brown and didn't match her black duty shoes and stockings. She had made her hair tidy and powdered her nose, but rushing down to the front door of the hospital she thought crossly that all the girls she knew would have refused flatly to go out looking so ridiculous; but there again, she reminded herself, Radinck considered she dressed deplorably anyway; he wouldn't notice.

If he did he said nothing, merely stowed her in the car and drove smoothly to Apsleys where they must have expected him, for they were attended to immediately by a quiet-voiced elderly man, who said very little as he displayed rings of every variety before them.

The Professor gave them a cursory glance. 'Choose which you prefer, Caroline,' he suggested. He sounded bored, and just for a moment resentment at his lack of interest at what should be an important event to them both almost choked her, but her common sense came to her rescue; why should he be interested? Buying the ring was to him only a necessary part of getting married. She picked a perfectly plain gold one and the man measured her finger and found her one to fit it before doing the same for the Professor. While he was away wrapping them up, Radinck said quietly: 'You aren't wearing your ring.'

'It's in the box in my pocket. I haven't had a chance—I mean, I can't wear it on duty and I forgot to wear it now—I'm not used to it yet.'

'Will you put it on?'

She did so, and when the man came back he saw it and smiled nicely at her. It made her feel much better and almost happy.

It hadn't taken much time: there was more than half an hour before she had to return to the ward, but when the Professor turned the car back in the direction of Oliver's she supposed that he had decided that there wasn't time for even a snack lunch and in all fairness she had said that she wouldn't mind missing her lunch. But in Cheapside he slowed the car, parked it and walked her into Le Poulbot where it seemed they were expected.

'I took the liberty of ordering for you since we have only a short time,' observed Radinck, 'filets de sole Leonora and a glass of white wine to go with it, and perhaps a sorbet.'

She was surprised at his thoughtfulness and stammered her thanks. 'But it means you have to rush over lunch too,' she pointed out.

'I'm not in the habit of sitting over my meals,' he observed. 'When one is by oneself it is a waste of time—one gets into bad habits…'

Caroline resolved silently to get him out of them even if it took her a lifetime and took care not to chat while they ate. Actually she longed to talk; there was so much she wanted to know, but she would have to wait: when he had made all the arrangements he would doubtless tell her. She was surprised when he asked: 'Which day do you wish to choose for the wedding?'

She said with some asperity: 'Well, how can I choose until I know when I'm to leave and when you want to go back to Holland?'

He waved aside the waiter and sat back to watch her eating her sorbet.

'Ah, yes—I saw your Senior Nursing Officer this morning. You may leave in five days' time—by then I shall have the licence, would any day after that suit you?'

She felt a surge of excitement at the very idea. 'That's…' she counted on her fingers, 'Sunday. Would Tuesday suit you? That would give me time to pack my things. Will you be here until then?'

He shook his head. 'I'm going back tomorrow—there are several patients I have to see. I'll come back on Sunday and see you then. Would you like to go to an hotel until the Tuesday?'

She was surprised again. 'That's very kind of you, but I'll stay in Meadow Road if you don't mind—Waterloo, you know.'

'Ah, yes, I had forgotten.' He glanced at his watch. 'We had better go.'

His leavetaking was casual. No one looking at the two of them, thought Caro, would have guessed that they were going to be married within a week. She watched him get into his car and drive away, her eyes filled with tears. She knew nothing about him; where he was staying, what he was doing in London, if he had friends…the only thing she was sure of was that she loved him enough to bear with his ways.

CHAPTER FOUR

FIVE DAYS, Caro discovered, could last for ever, especially when one didn't know what was going to happen at the end of them. The Professor had said he was going to see her on Sunday, but once again he had forgotten to mention time or place. True, she had enjoyed several hours of shopping which had left her very satisfied and reduced her nest egg to a few paltry pounds, all the same she wished very much that Sunday would come.

And finally come it did and Caro, burdened with a variety of presents from her friends and fellow nurses, left Oliver's early in the afternoon. She had several hours of overtime due to her and Sister Pringle, generous after her holiday, had told her to go early rather than wait until six o'clock. She had been surprised to find her staff nurse engaged and on the point of leaving, but she had been pleased too; Caro got on well with everyone in her quiet way and she would be missed. She would miss her life at Oliver's too, she thought, as she crossed the busy street in front of the forbidding exterior and made her way to Meadow Road, but she wasn't daunted at the idea of living in another country; she would have lived wherever Radinck was and not complained.

She fed Waterloo, made herself a pot of tea and spread her packages on the bed—an early morning tea-set from Stacey, Miriam and Clare, a tea-cosy from the nurses on the ward, a bright pink bath towel from the ward maid and the orderlies and some hand-kerchiefs from Sister Pringle, and over and above these, a cut glass vase from all her friends. She admired them at length, for with no family of her own, presents had been few and far between. After she had had her tea she went to the wardrobe and looked at the new clothes hanging there. Her wedding outfit, covered in a plastic wrapper, took up most of the room; it was a rather plain fine wool dress in a warm amber colour which, if the weather should prove cold, would go very well under her winter coat. She had bought a small velvet hat to go with it, rather expensive shoes and gloves and a leather handbag. Not even the Professor would be able to find fault with them, she considered. She had bought a suit too, a multi-coloured tweed with a Marks and Spencer sweater to go with it, and more shoes, a sensible pair for walking in, and new undies and slacks. She would have liked some new luggage to pack them in, but her case, although shabby, was quite adequate and she wanted a few pounds in her purse; Radinck had talked about an allowance in a cool voice which had made her determined not to make use of it until she was forced to.

He arrived just as she was making toast for her tea. The afternoon had turned wet and chilly and Caroline had drawn the curtains and got out the Fodor's Guide once more. She was sitting on the wool rug she had made for herself, the bread toasting on a fork, Waterloo sitting beside her, when Radinck thumped on the door. No one else thumped like that. She knew who it was and called to him to come in. She didn't get up but went on with her toast-making, saying merely: 'Hello, Radinck, would you like some tea? I'm just going to make it.'

'Thank you, that would be nice.' He took off his car coat and sat down in the shabby chair beside the fire.

'Have you just arrived?' she asked.

'Yes, they told me at Oliver's that you had left.' His eyes lighted on the presents still laid out on the divan and he looked a question.

'Wedding presents,' said Caro cheerfully, turning her toast. 'I've never had so many things all at once in my life.'

He said, 'Very nice,' and dismissed them. 'You are ready for Tuesday?'

'Yes, I think so.' She buttered the toast and got up to put the kettle on.

Radinck looked tired and even more severe than usual and so aloof that Caroline didn't dare to utter the words of sympathy crowding into her head. Instead she made the tea, poured him a cup and put it, with the toast, on a stool by his chair, and then set about making more toast.

Presently when he had drunk his tea and she had given him a second cup she asked in her soft voice: 'You haven't changed your mind? You really want me to marry you, Radinck? One often gets ideas that don't work out…'

'I still want to marry you, Caroline.' He had relaxed, leaning back eating his toast, stroking Waterloo who had got on to his knee. 'I thought that we might go out for dinner.'

'Thank you, that would be nice.'

'And tomorrow? I have to be at the hospital in the morning, but perhaps we might go out in the afternoon. You have finished your shopping?'

'Yes, thank you—I have only to pack.'

He nodded. 'They are all delighted at Huis Thoe. You realise that we have to return by the night boat on Tuesday?'

'Yes.' She bit into her toast, trying to think of something to add and couldn't. She was astonished when he asked:

'What is the colour of your dress?'

'The one I've bought for the wedding? I suppose you'd call it dark amber.' She took a sip of tea and went on: 'I know you aren't interested in what I wear, it's a very plain dress—quite nice, you know, but no one's likely to take a second look at me, if you see what I mean.'

He raised his thick eyebrows. 'And is that your ambition? I have always understood that women— especially young ones—like to be noticed.'

'Not with a face like mine, they wouldn't,' Caro assured him.

He eyed her gravely. 'Your figure is not displeasing,' he observed, and sounded almost as surprised at his words as she was.

He didn't have to wait on the landing this time. She had adopted the old-fashioned idea of wearing her best clothes on Sundays even if she wasn't going anywhere; it made the day seem a little different from all the others, so she was ready when Radinck suggested that they should go.

This time he took her to the Connaught Hotel Restaurant and because it was Sunday evening her green wool dress didn't seem too out of place, and she really wouldn't have minded; she had the sapphire on her finger, proclaiming that she had some sort of claim on her companion—although judging by the looks she received from some of the younger women sitting near them, it wasn't at all justified—besides, she was hungry. She did full justice to the cheese soufflé—as light as air, followed by filets de sole princesse and rounded off by millefeuille from the sweet trolley, all nicely helped down by the champagne the Professor had ordered. Caro wasn't very used to champagne; she wasn't sure if she liked it, but with the second glass she assured her companion that it was a drink which grew on one, and although she hadn't intended to make him laugh, he actually did.

She spent the next morning packing her clothes and putting her small treasures and ornaments, carefully wrapped, into a large cardboard box.

She was quite ready when Radinck called for her, dressed in the new suit, her face carefully made up. It was most gratifying when he remarked casually: 'You look nice—is that new?'

She told him yes, reflecting that it had been worth the scandalous price she had paid for it at Jaegers; a lukewarm compliment but still a compliment.

They went to the Connaught again and when she observed how very nice it was, the Professor agreed pleasantly enough. 'I stay here if I'm in England for a few days,' he told her, and she fell to wondering where he went if his stay was protracted. Her thoughts must have been mirrored on her face, for after a pause he said:

'I have a small house in Essex, but it is hardly worth going there unless I'm over for a week or more.'

'What exactly do you do?' she asked carefully. 'That's if you don't mind telling me.'

He didn't answer her at once but remarked testily: 'Why is it that so many remarks you make appear to put me in the wrong, Caroline?' and before she could deny this: 'I am a physician, specialising in heart conditions, and the various diseases consequent to them.'

'But you lecture?'

'Yes.'

'And of course you're a consultant as well. Do you travel a great deal?'

He frowned a little. 'What a great many questions, Caroline!'

She agreed cheerfully. 'But you see, Radinck, if I ask them now, you'll never have to answer them again, will you?'

'That is true. I hope you don't expect to travel with me? I'm used to being alone—I concentrate better.'

She eyed him with pity wringing her heart, but all she said was: 'Of course I don't—I haven't forgotten that I'm to be a sheet anchor.'

He gave her a hard suspicious look which she met with a clear friendly gaze.

She hadn't asked what they were doing with the rest of the afternoon. She expected to be taken to Meadow Road, but it seemed that Radinck had other plans, for after lunch he left the car at the hotel and hailed a taxi. It cost Caro a great effort not to ask him where they were going, but she guessed that he was waiting for her to do just that. In the taxi he said: 'I have a wedding gift for you, but I wish you to see it first—it may not please you.'

She would have been a moron not to have been pleased, she thought presently, standing in front of the triple mirror in an exclusive furrier's shop. Mink, no less—ranch mink, he had carefully explained, because he thought that a coat made from trapped animals might distress her. It was a perfect fit, and when she remarked upon this he had told her casually that Clare had very kindly supplied her measurements.

She thanked him quietly and sincerely, careful to do it while the sales lady wasn't there. 'I can wear it tomorrow,' she told him. 'I was going to wear my winter coat…'

She understood then that for his wife to return to Huis Thoe in anything less than a mink coat would have upset everyone's idea of the fitness of things. She reflected with some excitement that she would be expected to dress very well, go to the hairdressers too and use the kind of make-up advertised so glossily in *Harpers* and *Vogue*. It struck her then that she was going to be a baroness—ridiculous but true. Just for a moment she quailed at the thought, but then her sensible head told her that it didn't matter what either of them were if they could love each other—and she already did that; it was just a question of getting Radinck to fall in love with her. She wasn't quite sure how she was going to do it, but it would be done.

Leaving the shop Radinck observed: 'I hope you will be pleased. I thought it would be pleasant if we gave a small dinner party for your friends and Sir Eustace and my best man this evening. At the hotel in my rooms there; we shall have to leave directly after we have been married tomorrow, so there is no question of giving a lunch party then.'

'How nice,' said Caro faintly. 'C-can I wear this dress?'

'Certainly not. It will be black ties—your three friends are wearing long dresses. Have you no evening gown?'

She shook her head. 'Well, no—you see I don't go out a great deal.' Not at all, she added silently, but pride stopped her from saying so aloud.

'In that case tell me where you would like to buy a dress and we'll go there now.'

'Oh, I couldn't…'

He said coolly: 'Don't be so old-fashioned, Caroline—it is perfectly permissible for a man to buy his future wife a dress should he wish to do so. We will go to Fortnum and Mason.'

Caro goggled at him. 'But I've never been there in my life—not to buy anything.'

'Then it's time you did.'

He was there and she was getting out of the car before she could think of any argument against this and was led unresisting to the Dress Department where the Professor, looking more severe than ever, was instantly attended to by the head sales lady.

Having made his wishes clear he took himself off to a comfortable chair and left Caro to be led away by the sales lady to go through a selection of dresses which were all so stunning that she had no idea what she wanted.

It was the sales lady who pointed out that green was a good colour for hazel eyes and furthermore she had just the thing to suit, and if that wasn't to madam's taste, there was a charming honey-coloured crêpe or a grey crêpe de Chine...

Caro, almost delirious with excitement, tried them all on in turn and settled for the green; organza over silk with full sleeves gathered into tight buttoned cuffs and a low ruffled neckline. And when the sales lady suggested that she might like some rather pretty sandals to go with it, she agreed recklessly. She told Radinck about the sandals as they left the shop. 'I had no evening shoes,' she explained gravely, 'so I hope you don't mind. They were rather expensive.'

She hadn't been able to discover the price of the dress; the sales lady had been vague and she had watched Radinck sign a cheque without showing any signs of shock. She hoped that it hadn't been too expensive, but it wasn't until later that evening while she was dressing that she saw its label; a couture garment, and her mind boggled at the cost.

They had tea presently in a tiny shop all gilt and white paint, with the most heavenly cakes Caro had ever eaten, and on the way back she thanked him fervently and then went scarlet when he said coldly: 'You have no need to be quite so fulsome in your thanks. I have hardly lavished a fortune upon you, Caroline.'

She turned her head and looked out of the car window, wanting to burst into tears; the last thing she must ever do before him. She said brightly, proud of her steady voice, 'How dark it grows in the afternoons—but I like winter, don't you?'

She didn't see his quick glance at her averted face. 'You will be able to skate on the canal near Huis Thoe if it freezes enough.' His voice was casual and quite different from the biting tones he had just used. Caroline supposed she would learn in time—not to mind when he snubbed her, not to mind when he was cold and distant; there would surely be times when they could talk together, get to know each other. It would take time, but after all, he had said that he liked her.

He had to go back to the hospital that evening. He left her at Meadow Road, said that he would call for her at half past seven and drove away, leaving her to tell Waterloo all about it, wash her hair, do her face and put on the new dress. She had been ready and waiting half an hour or more before he returned, pleased with her appearance and hoping that he would be pleased too.

His cool 'very nice!' when he arrived was rather less than she had hoped for and his further: 'The dress is pretty,' although truthful, hardly flattered her, but she thanked him politely, tucked Waterloo up in his box and picked up the new fur coat. It was almost frightening how the touch of his cool hands on her shoulders as he held it for her sent her insides seesaw-ing.

The evening was a great success; Clare, Miriam and Stacey had been fetched by the best man whose name Caro, in her excitement, didn't catch, although she remembered afterwards that he had said that he had an English wife who had just had a baby, and Sir Eustace and his wife arrived a few minutes after them. They all looked very elegant, Caro consid-ered, drinking champagne cocktails in the elegant room Radinck had taken her to; her friends did credit to the occasion and sadly seemed on better terms with their host than she did. Just as he did with them. It was strange, she mused a little cloudily because of the champagne, that he should want to marry her when she never amused him, but there again, she couldn't imagine any of them allowing him to lead the quiet, studious life he seemed to enjoy. But her low spirits didn't last for long; the ring was admired, as was the coat, and her friends' pleasure at her change of fortune was genuine enough. And Lady Jenkins, under the impression that it was a love match and knowing that Caro had no parents, became quite motherly.

They dined late and at leisure at the round table set up in the Professor's sitting room at the hotel. Iced melon was followed by lobster thermidor and rounded off with ices, trifle and charlotte russe. They drank champagne and over coffee the Professor observed that it hardly seemed right to have a wedding cake before the wedding, but he had done his best to substitute that with petits fours, covered in white icing and decorated with silver leaves and flowers.

It was almost midnight when the party broke up and everyone went home, cracking jokes about seeing them at the church in the morning. When they had all gone, Caro put on her coat once more and was driven back to Meadow Road, making polite conversation all the way. She only stopped when Radinck remarked: 'You're very chatty—it must be the champagne.'

He didn't sound annoyed, though, only a little bored, so she said, 'Yes, I expect it is,' and lapsed into silence until they reached the house. He got out first, opened her door and went with her up the stairs, to take the key from her hand and open the door. The contrast after the spacious elegance of the hotel room was cruel, but he didn't say anything, only gave her back her key, cautioned her to be ready when he came for her in the morning and wished her goodnight.

'Goodnight,' said Caro hurriedly, because she hadn't thanked him yet and he seemed in a hurry to be gone. 'It was a delightful dinner party, thank you, Radinck.' And when he muttered something she added: 'I'll be ready when you come.'

She smiled at him and shut the door quite briskly, leaving him on the landing. She loved him so very much, but she mustn't let that weaken her resolve to alter his stern outlook on life. She suspected that he was a man who had always had his own way, even to shutting a door when he wanted to and not a moment before. A small beginning, but she had to start somewhere.

She slept dreamlessly with Waterloo curled up in a tight ball on her feet and was up much earlier than she needed to be, and true to her word, she was dressed and ready when Radinck came for her. Waterloo and her luggage were to be collected after the ceremony. Caroline cast a look round the little room and followed Radinck down the stairs to the car. The drive to the church was a short one and they hardly spoke. At the door she was handed over to Sir Eustace waiting in the porch and given a small bouquet of rich yellow roses which the Professor took from the back of the car. He nodded briefly at her and just for a moment she panicked, staring up at him with eyes full of doubt, and he must have seen that, for he smiled suddenly and she glimpsed the man under the calm mask and all her doubts went. If he could smile like that once, he could do it again, and she would make sure that he did. She took Sir Eustace's arm and walked firmly down the aisle to where Radinck, towering over everything in sight, waited for her.

She had no clear recollection of the ceremony. The best man had given her an encouraging smile as she reached Radinck's side, but the Professor didn't look at her at all. Indeed, he looked rather grim during the short service. Only as he put the ring on her finger he smiled slightly. She wanted to smile too, but she didn't; she would have to remember to remain friendly and undemanding quite without romantic feelings; he didn't hold with romance. That was something else which she had to alter.

There was to be no wedding breakfast. Everyone

said goodbye in the church porch and Caro got into the car beside Radinck, not feeling in the least married and resolved to change his life for him. Indeed when Clare put her head through the window and exclaimed: 'Good lord, you're a baroness now!' she started to deny it and then declared: 'I'd forgotten that— Oh, dear!' She looked so woebegone at the idea that Clare laughed at her.

The Professor didn't intend to waste time; Caro's luggage was put in the boot, Waterloo, in a travelling basket, was arranged on the back seat, and with a hurried word to Mrs Hodge, who looked aggrieved because it hadn't been a proper wedding at all, Caro settled herself tidily beside the Professor. Afterwards, she had no very clear recollection of the journey either. They travelled by Hovercraft from Dover and although they stopped for lunch and again for tea, she had no idea what they had talked about or what she had eaten. The Professor had laid himself out to be pleasant and she had been careful not to chat, answering him when he made some observation but refraining from discussing the morning's ceremony. It was he who asked her if she had been pleased with her wedding, in much the same manner as someone asking if she had enjoyed her lunch, and she told him yes, it had been very nice—a colourless statement, but she could think of nothing better to say. She did enquire the name of the best man and was told he was Tiele Raukema van den Eck, not long married to an English girl. 'You must meet her,' suggested the Professor casually. 'She's rather a nice little thing—they've just had a son.'

It seemed there was no more to be said on the subject. Caro sat quietly as they sped northward and wondered if Noakes and the other servants would be glad to see her. Radinck had said that they had missed her, but going back as the lady of the house was quite a different kettle of fish.

She need not have worried. They were greeted with wide smiles and a great deal of handshaking and when that was done, Noakes led them into the drawing room where, on a small circular table in the centre of the room, was a wedding cake. Caro stopped short and gave a delighted laugh. 'Radinck, how kind of you to think of…'

She looked at him, still laughing, and saw at once that she had been mistaken. He was as surprised as she was—it must have been Noakes.

He was standing in the doorway with Juffrouw Kropp and Marta and the others grouped around him, waiting to be praised like eager children. Caro hoped that they hadn't heard her speak to Radinck; she turned to them now. 'Noakes, all of you—what a wonderful surprise! We're both thrilled; it is the most beautiful cake. Thank you—all of you.' She went on recklessly: 'I'm going to cut it now and we'll all have a piece with some champagne. We were going to have the champagne anyway, weren't we, Radinck?'

She turned a smiling face towards him, her eyes beseeching him to act the part of a happy bridegroom. After all, it was only for once; every other night he could go to his study and spend the evenings with his books.

He met her look with a mocking smile she hoped no one else saw. 'But certainly we will drink champagne,' he agreed. 'Noakes, fetch up half a dozen bottles and get someone to set out the glasses. And thank you all for this magnificent cake.' He repeated it all in Dutch and there was handclapping and smiling and a good deal of bustling to and fro until the champagne had been brought and they went to cut the cake. Caroline, handed the knife by Noakes and alone with the Professor at the table for a moment, said softly; 'I'm afraid it's the custom for us both to hold the knife...'

His hand felt cool and quite impersonal and touched her only briefly. He was disliking the happy little ceremony very much, she knew that; perhaps it reminded him of his first wedding. He'd been in love then...

They ate the cake and drank the champagne and presently Juffrouw Kropp took Caroline upstairs to her room to tidy herself for dinner. It was a different bedroom this time; a vast apartment in the front of the house with an equally vast bed with a brocade coverlet to match the blue curtains and beautiful Hepplewhite furniture. A bathroom led from it and on the other side a dressing room, another bathroom and another bedroom, all leading one to another. Juffrouw Kropp beamed and smiled before she went away, and left alone, Caro explored more thoroughly; it was all very splendid but comfortable too. She tidied herself, did her hair and went downstairs again to join Radinck in the drawing-room, where they made conversation over their drinks before going in to dinner.

Marta had excelled herself with little spinach tarts, roast duckling with black cherries and a bombe surprise. Caro, desperately maintaining a conversation about nothing much, ate some of everything although she had no appetite, because Marta would be upset to see her lovely dishes returned to the kitchen half eaten, and she drank the hock Noakes poured for them, a little too much of it, which was a good thing because it made her feel falsely cheerful.

They had their coffee in the drawing-room and Noakes went away with a benign smile which drew down the corners of the Professor's mouth so that Caro, now valiant with too much drink, said cheerfully: 'You've hated every minute of it, haven't you, Radinck? But I'm going to my room in a few minutes, only before I go I'd like to thank you for giving me such a nice wedding.' She added kindly: 'It's only this one evening, you know, you won't have to do it ever again. You asked me not to disturb your life, and I won't, only they all expected...' She pinkened faintly. 'Well, they expected us to look—like...'

'Exactly, Caroline.' He had got to his feet. 'I'm only sorry that I didn't think of the wedding cake.' He smiled at her: it was a kind, gentle sort of smile and it held a touch of impatience. She said goodnight without fuss and didn't linger. She thought about that smile later, as she got ready for bed. It had been a glimpse of Radinck again, only next time, she promised herself, he would smile without impatience. It might take a long time, but that was something she had.

She woke early while it was still almost dark. She had opened the door to the verandah outside her room before she got into her enormous bed, and Waterloo, after a long sound sleep on her feet after his lengthy journey and hearty supper, was prowling up and down it, talking to her. She got up, put on her new quilted dressing gown and slippers and went to join him.

The sky was getting paler every minute, turning pink along the horizon; it was going to be a lovely November day, bright and frosty. Somewhere Caroline could hear Rex barking and the sound of horses' hooves and then Radinck's whistle to the dog. So that was what he did before breakfast. She vowed then and there to learn to ride.

One of the maids, Ilke, brought her her early morning tea presently, and told her smilingly that breakfast would be at half past eight, or would she rather have it in bed?

Caro elected to go downstairs. She had never had her breakfast in bed, for there had been no one to bring it to her, and the idea didn't appeal to her very much. She bathed and put on her suit and one of the Marks and Spencer sweaters and went down to the hall. It was absurd, but she wasn't sure where she was to breakfast. When she had been staying in the house she had seen only the library, the drawing-room and the dining-room, but there were several more doors and passages leading from the hall and she had no idea where they led. She need not have fussed; Noakes was waiting to conduct her to a small, cosy room leading off the hall, where there was a bright fire burning and a table laid ready for her. Of the Professor there was no sign and she thought it might sound silly if she asked Noakes where he was, so she bade him a smiling good morning, and while she made a good breakfast, listened to his carefully put advice.

'There's Juffrouw Kropp waiting ter show yer the 'ouse, ma'am, and then Marta 'opes yer'll go to the kitchens and take a look at the menu, and anything yer wants ter know yer just ask me. We're all that 'appy that yer're 'ere, ma'am.'

'Noakes, you're very kind to say so, and I'm happy too. When I've found my feet we must have some more singing—I still think we should do something about Christmas, don't you?' She remembered something. 'And, Noakes, I want your help. Is there someone who can teach me to ride? I—I want to surprise the Professor.'

His cheerful face spread into a vast smile. 'Now ain't that just the ticket—the Professor, 'e rides a treat, great big 'orse 'e's got, too, but there's a pony as is 'ardly used. Old Jan'll know—I'll get 'im to come and see yer and I'll come wiv 'im.'

'Thank you, Noakes—it must be a secret, though.' Caroline finished her coffee and got up from the table. 'I'm going to fetch Waterloo and take him round the house with Juffrouw Kropp, then he'll feel at home. Where's Rex?'

'Gone with the Professor. Most days 'e does, ma'am.'

It took all of two hours to go over the house. She hadn't realised quite how big it was, with a great many little passages leading to small rooms, and funny twisted stairs from one floor to the next as well as the massive front staircase. She would have got lost if it hadn't been for Juffrouw Kropp, leading her from one room to the next, waiting patiently while she examined its contents, and then explaining them in basic Dutch so that Caro had at least some idea of them. They were all beautifully furnished and well-kept, but as far as she could make out, never used. A house full of guests, she dreamed to herself, all laughing and talking and dancing in the evening in that lovely drawing-room and riding out in the mornings, with her riding even better than the best there. She sighed and Juffrouw Kropp asked her if she were tired, and when she shook her head in vigorous denial, preceded her downstairs to visit the glories on the ground floor.

The drawing-room she knew, also the library and the morning-room. Now she was conducted round a second sitting-room, furnished with deep armchairs, a work table from the Regency period, several lamp tables and two bow-fronted display cabinets. A lovely room, but not used, she felt sure. Well, she would use it. There was a billiard room too, a garden room and a small room furnished with a desk and chair and several filing cabinets—used by the secretary, Caroline supposed. There was a luxurious cloakroom too and a great many large cupboards as well as several rooms lined with shelves and a pantry or two.

She hoped she would remember where each of them was if ever she needed it, although she couldn't think why she should. The first floor had been easy enough; her own room and the adjoining ones took up half the front corridor and most of one side, and the half a dozen bedrooms and their bathrooms on that floor took up the rest of its space; the smaller rooms and passages she would have to explore later.

She drank her coffee presently, concentrating on what she had seen, reminding herself that it was hers now as well as Radinck's and he would expect her to be responsible for his home. She had no intention of usurping Juffrouw Kropp's position, but it was obvious that even that experienced lady expected her to give orders from time to time.

The kitchens she already knew, but now it was a question of poking her mousy head into all the cupboards and lobbies and dressers while it was explained to her what was in all of them and then, finally, she was given a seat at the kitchen table and offered the day's menu. Noakes translated it for her while Marta waited anxiously to see if she would approve, and when that had been done to everyone's satisfaction, Noakes led her back to the smaller sitting-room, where she had decided to spend her leisure and where after a few minutes Jan was admitted.

Noakes had to act as go-between, of course, but Jan agreed readily enough to teaching her. The pony, he agreed with Noakes, was just right since the Baroness was small and light. Caro, who had forgot-

ten that she was a baroness, felt a little glow of pleasure at his words. They decided that she should begin
the very next morning, and well pleased with herself,
she got her coat and took herself off for a walk.

She lunched alone, since the Professor didn't
come home, and in the afternoon she curled up in the
library and had another go at her Dutch. She would
have to have lessons, for she was determined to learn
to speak it as quickly as possible, but in the mean-
time she could at least look up as many words as she
could. She and Juffrouw Kropp were to go through
the linen cupboard on the following morning. She
would make her companion say everything in her
own language and she would repeat it after her; she
would learn a lot that way. And tomorrow she would
get Noakes to drive her into Leeuwarden so that she
could buy some wool and fill her time with knitting.
More flowers about the house too, she decided, and
an hour's practice at the piano each day. There was
more than enough to keep her busy.

She went upstairs to change after her solitary tea;
she put on her wedding dress again and then went to
the drawing-room to wait for Radinck, taking a book
with her so that it wouldn't look as though she had
been there ages, expecting him.

When he did get home, only a short time before
dinner, she wished him a cheerful good evening, vol-
unteered no information as to her day, hoped that he

had had a good one himself and took up her book again. He had stressed that she wasn't to interfere with his way of living and she would abide by it. She accepted a drink from him and when he excused himself on the plea of work to do before dinner, assured him that she didn't mind in the least.

They met at the dinner table presently and over an unhurried meal talked comfortably enough about this and that, and as they got up to go into the drawing-room for their coffee Caro said diffidently: 'Don't come into the drawing-room unless you want to, Radinck. I'll get Noakes to bring coffee to your study.'

He followed her into the room and closed the door. He said irritably: 'I'll take my coffee where I wish to, Caroline. I'm sure you mean well, but kindly don't interfere.' He glared down at her. 'I shall be going out very shortly.'

Her voice was quite serene. 'Yes, Radinck. Do you like your coffee black?' She poured it with a steady hand and went to sit down, telling herself she wasn't defeated, only discouraged.

CHAPTER FIVE

THE DAYS PASSED, piling themselves into a week. Caro, awake early as usual by reason of Waterloo's soliloquy as he paced the balcony, sat herself up against her lace-trimmed pillows and began to assess the progress she had made in that time. Nothing startling, she conceded, ticking off her small successes first: her riding lessons had proved well worth the effort. She had got on to Jemmy, the pony, each morning under Jan's eagle eye and done her best while her tutor muttered and tutted at her and occasionally took her to task in a respectful manner, while the faithful Noakes translated every word. And she had learned the geography of the house, having gone over it several times by herself and once or twice with Juffrouw Kropp, learning the names of the various pieces of furniture from that good lady.

She had applied herself to her Dutch too; even though she had little idea how to converse in that language she had worried her way through a host of useful words. Besides all this, she had got Noakes to drive her to Leeuwarden, where she had bought wool and a pattern and started on a sweater for Radinck's Christmas present; probably he would never wear it, but she was getting a lot of pleasure from knitting it, although as the instructions were in Dutch she had had to guess at a good deal of the pattern and enlist Juffrouw Kropp's help over the more difficult bits.

Her eyes fell on Waterloo, who having finished his early morning exercise, was sitting in the doorway washing his elderly face; he at least was happy with the whole house to roam and a safe outdoors with no traffic threatening his safety, and she shared his opinion. The grounds round the house were large and beyond the red-brick wall which encompassed them were water meadows and quiet lanes and bridle paths. Caroline had roamed at will during the week, finding her way around, going to the village where she was surprised to be greeted by its inhabitants. She still found it strange to be addressed as Baroness and she had had a struggle to answer civilly in Dutch, but smiling and nodding went a long way towards establishing a sort of rapport.

But with Radinck she had made no progress at all. He was polite, remote and continued to live his own life, just as though she wasn't there. True, once or twice he had discussed some interesting point regarding his work with her, asked her casually if she had been to the village and informed her that now their marriage had been put in the *Haagsche Post* and *Elseviers* they might expect visitors and some invitations, and had gone on to suggest that she might like to go to Leeuwarden or Groningen and buy herself some clothes, and the following morning his secretary had given her a cheque book with a slip of paper inside it on which the Professor had scrawled: Your allowance will be paid into the bank quarterly. The sum he had written had left Caroline dumbfounded.

But it was early days yet, she reminded herself cheerfully. He would be surprised and, she hoped, delighted to discover that she could ride. The last thing she wanted to happen was for him to feel ashamed of her because of her social shortcomings, even if he didn't want her as a wife she would manage his home just as he wanted it, entertain his friends and learn to live his way of life. She owed him that, and never mind how impatient and irritable he became.

She drank her morning tea and presently went downstairs to her breakfast, to stop in the doorway of the breakfast room. Radinck was sitting at the table, a cup of coffee in one hand, a letter he was reading in the other.

He got up when he saw her, pulled out a chair and

said politely: 'Do sit down; I forgot to tell you yesterday that I have given myself a day off. I thought we might go down to den Haag so that you can do some shopping. My mother always got her things from Le Bonneterie there—it's rather like a small Harrods, and you might possibly like it—if not, we can try somewhere else.'

Caroline didn't like to mention that she had never bought anything in Harrods. She agreed happily; a whole day in his company, even if he had nothing much to say to her, would be heaven, but here she was to be disappointed, for in the car, racing across the Afsluitdijk, he mentioned casually that he had a consultation at the Red Cross Hospital in den Haag and after leaving her at Le Bonneterie he would rejoin her there an hour or so later. 'I daresay it will take you that time to buy your clothes. I suggest that you get a sheepskin jacket and some boots—it can be cold once the winter comes.'

Caroline started doing sums in her head; her allowance was a generous one but she had no idea how much good clothes cost in Holland. She would need several dresses, she supposed, and more separates and some evening clothes.

'You're very silent,' remarked Radinck presently.

'Well, I was just thinking what I needed to buy. Would two evening dresses do?'

'Certainly not—there will be a hospital ball in

Leeuwarden in a few weeks' time, and another one in Groningen and any number of private parties. At Christmas I invite a number of guests to the house, but before then we will have an evening reception so that you meet my friends.'

She had to get this straight. 'But you like to lead a quiet life; you told me so—you like to work and read in the evenings. You'll only be inviting them because of me.'

'That is so.' They were flying down the E-10 and there was plenty to capture her interest, only she had too much on her mind.

'Yes, but don't you see?' she persisted in her quiet voice, 'you're having to do something you don't want to do.' She went on quickly, looking straight ahead of her, 'You don't have to do it for me, you know. I'm—I'm very happy—besides, I'd feel scared at meeting so many strange people.'

'Once you have met them they won't be strange.' The calm logic of his voice made her want to stamp her feet with temper. 'And to revert to our discussion, I suggest that you buy several dresses of a similar sort to the one you wore at our wedding.' He glanced sideways at her. 'The suit you are wearing is nice, why not get another one like it? And some casual clothes, of course.'

Caroline said tartly: 'Do you want me to change my hairstyle too? It could be tinted and cut and permed and...'

'You will leave your hair exactly as it is.' He added stiffly, 'I like it the way you wear it.'

She was so surprised that she asked quite meekly: 'How much money am I to spend? I could get a great deal with about half of my allowance.' She frowned. 'And will they take my cheque? They don't know me from Adam.'

'I shall go with you. You will have no difficulty in writing cheques for anything you want, Caroline, but this time you will leave me to pay the bill when I come to fetch you.'

'Oh—all right, and I'll pay you back afterwards.'

'I do not wish to be repaid. Caroline, did I not tell you that I was a rich man?'

'No—at least I can't remember that you did. You did say that there was plenty of money, but I don't suppose that's the same as being rich, is it?'

A muscle twitched at the corner of the Professor's firm mouth. 'No,' he agreed quietly, 'it's not quite the same.'

They were in the heavily populated area of the country now, for he had turned away from Amsterdam and was working his way round the city to pick up the motorway to den Haag on its southern side. As they took the road past Leiden which would lead them to the heart of den Haag, Caro said: 'It's very pretty here and there are some beautiful houses, only I like yours much better.'

'Ours,' Radinck reminded her.

The city was full of traffic and people and a bewildering number of narrow streets. The Professor wove his way into the heart of the shopping centre and turned away down a side street to stop after a moment or two before a large shop with elegantly dressed windows. It was quiet there, the houses all round it were old and there were few people about, and Caro took a deep breath of pure pleasure at the thought of spending the next hour or two in the dignified building, spending money without having to count every penny before she did so.

The Professor was known there. An elderly woman with a kind face listened carefully to what he had to say, smiled and nodded and without giving Caro time to do more than say, 'Goodbye,' led her away.

The next hour or so was blissful: Caro, guided discreetly by the elderly lady, became the possessor of a sheepskin jacket because Radinck had told her to buy one, a suit—dogtooth check with a short jacket and a swinging pleated skirt—three Italian print dresses and a finely pleated georgette jersey twopiece because although she didn't think she needed it she couldn't bear not to have it, a dashing bolero and skirt with a silk blouse to go with them and four evening dresses: she would probably never wear more than one of them despite what Radinck had said, but it was hard to call a halt, especially with the elderly lady egging her on in her more than adequate English. And then there was the question of suitable shoes, stockings to go with them, gloves, a little mink hat to go with her coat, and since it seemed a shame not to buy them while she had the opportunity, undies. She was wandering back from that department and had stopped to examine the baby clothes in the children's department when Radinck joined her. She flushed under his mocking eyes and said defensively: 'I was on my way back. They're adding it up—the bill, I mean—I had a few minutes...'

She put down the muslin garment she had been admiring and walked past him. 'It's a lovely shop,' she told him chattily to cover her awkwardness. 'I've bought an awful lot. Did you have a successful consultation?'

He gave some non-committal answer, made some remark to the sales lady and then studied the bill. Caro, watching his face, was unable to discover his feelings about it. His expression gave nothing away, although the total was such that if it had been handed to her she would have screamed at the amount.

But he didn't mention it. The packages and boxes loaded into the boot, Caroline was invited to get into the car, and within ten minutes she found herself in a small, very smart restaurant, drinking a sherry and eyeing a menu with an appetite sharpened by its contents. And not only did Radinck not mention it, but he talked. He told her about the hospital where he had been that morning and the patients he had seen, he even discussed the conditions he had been asked to examine. Just for a while the bland mask slipped a little and Caro, always a good listener, became a perfect one, listening intelligently, asking the right question at the right moment and never once venturing an opinion of her own, and she got her reward, for presently he observed: 'You must forgive me, I am so used to being alone—I have been uttering my thoughts and you must have been bored.'

'No, I wasn't,' said Caro forthrightly. 'I'm interested—you forget that I'm a nurse, but there are bits I don't quite understand. You were telling me about Fröhlich's syndrome—I can't quite see how hypophosphatisia can't be medically treated—if it's just a question of calcium...'

The Professor put down his coffee cup. 'Well, it's like this...'

For a bridegroom of rather more than a week, his conversation was hardly flattering: she might have been sitting there, wearing a sack and a false nose, but to Caro, it was the thin—very thin—edge of the wedge.

Back home again she went straight to her room with one of the maids bearing her various parcels.

Radinck was going out again and she hoped he might tell her where, but in this she was disappointed. He was leaving the house without a word before she had reached the top of the staircase. She consoled herself by trying on every single thing she had bought, and it was only as she took off the last of the evening dresses that she remembered her day-dream—playing to Radinck in a lovely pink dress, and none of the dresses were pink; she would have to go to den Haag again and buy one. Meanwhile she might do a little practising while she waited for him to come back.

He wasn't coming. Noakes met her in the hall with the news that the Professor had just telephoned to say that he wouldn't be back for dinner, and Caroline, anxious to keep her end up, said airily: 'Oh, yes, Noakes, he did say he might have to stay. I'll have mine on a tray, please, and if none of you have anything better to do, shall we get together over those carols presently?'

She was so disappointed that she could eat hardly any of the delicious food Noakes brought presently, and even though she told herself she was a fool to have expected Radinck to have changed his ways all at once, she was hard put to it to preserve a cheerful face. It helped, of course, discussing the carols with Noakes and Marta and Juffrouw Kropp and the others. She sat at the piano, trying out the various tunes to find those they knew—and when they had, she was thrilled to discover that they sang rather well. With the aid of Noakes and her dictionary, she prevailed upon some of them to sing in harmony—it was a bit ragged, but there were several weeks to go to Christmas and if Radinck was going to be away most evenings, there was ample time to rehearse.

She made herself think about her new wardrobe and the carols as she got ready for bed, banishing Radinck from her mind. Easier said than done: he kept popping up all over the place.

It was after breakfast the following morning that he telephoned her to say that he was going to Brussels and wouldn't be back until the next day, late in the evening. 'So don't wait up for me,' his voice sounded cool over the wire. 'I haven't got Rex with me, so would you mind walking him—once a day will do, he is very adaptable.'

Caroline made her voice equally cool; rather like an efficient secretary's. 'Of course.' She wanted to tell him to take care of himself, to ask what he was going to do in Brussels, but she didn't; she said goodbye in a cheerful voice and rang off.

The day went by on leaden feet. Not even her riding lesson raised her spirits, although she was doing quite well now, trotting sedately round and round the field nearest the stables, with Rex keeping pace with Jemmy. He did the same thing again on the following morning, taking upon himself the role of companion and pacemaker, and because the weather was changing with thunderous skies swallowing the chilly blue, Caroline spent the afternoon in the library, conning her Dutch and knitting away at the sweater, with Waterloo and Rex for company, and because she had to keep up appearances, she changed into one of her new dresses that evening and dined alone at the big table, feeling lost but not allowing that to show, and after an hour working away at the carols again she went up to her room, meeting Noakes' enquiry as to whether she knew at what time the Professor would be back with a serene: 'He said late, Noakes, and I wasn't to wait up. I should lock up if he's not back by eleven o'clock—ask Marta to leave a thermos jug of coffee out, would you?'

It was long after midnight when the Professor returned. Caro, lying wide awake in her bed, heard the gentle growl of the car and saw its lights flash past her windows and presently her husband's firm tread coming up the stairs and going past her door. Only then did she curl up into a ball with Waterloo as close as he could get and sleep.

It was raining when she awoke, and cold and dark as well. None of these mattered, though. Radinck was home again and she might even see him before he left the house—perhaps he would be at breakfast.

She got dressed in the new suit and the wildly expensive brogue shoes she had bought to go with it, and went downstairs.

He wasn't there, and Noakes, remarking on her early appearance, observed, 'Back late, wasn't 'e, ma'am? I 'eard him come in—ever so quiet.'

'Yes, I know, though I was still awake, Noakes.'

'Pity 'e 'ad ter go again so early—no proper rest. 'E works too 'ard.'

'Yes, Noakes, I know he does.' She gave the elderly face a sweet smile. 'Noakes, it's too wet for me to go riding, I suppose?'

'Lor', yes, ma'am—best stay indoors. Juffrouw Kropp wanted to ask about some curtains that want renewing.'

'I'll see her after breakfast and then go to the kitchens.'

It was still only ten o'clock by the time she had fulfilled her household duties and the rain had lessened a little. 'I'm going for a walk,' she told Noakes. 'I won't take Rex with me and I won't go far—I just feel like some exercise.'

She put her new hooded raincoat on over the new suit, found her gloves and let herself out of a side door. The rain was falling steadily and there was a snarling wind, but they suited her mood. She walked briskly across the gardens, into the fields behind the wall, and joined the country lane, leading away to a village in the distance. She had walked barely half a mile when she saw a slow-moving group coming towards her—a cart drawn by a stout pony and surrounded by a family of tinkers. They were laughing and shouting to each other, not minding the weather, carefree and happy. Except for a small donkey tied to the back of the cart; it wasn't only wet, it was in a shocking condition, its ribs starting through its dirty matted coat, and it was heavily in foal. It was being ruthlessly beaten with a switch wielded by a shambling youth, and Caro, now abreast of the whole party, cried 'Stop!' so furiously that they did. She took the switch from the youth and flung it into the canal by the side of the lane, then she mustered her Dutch. '*Hoeveel?*' she asked imperiously, pointing at the deplorable beast, and then with a flash of inspiration, she pointed to herself and added: 'Baroness Thoe van Erckelens.'

She was pleased to see that the name meant something to them. The leader of the party, a scruffy middle-aged man, gave her a respectful look, even if a bit doubtful. Caroline had to dispel the doubt; she turned and pointed again, this time towards Huis Thoe, just visible behind its high wall. While they were all staring at it she went over to the dejected little beast and began to untie the rope round its neck, and when they would have stopped her, held up a firm little hand. '*Ik koop,*' she told them, and waved

towards the house, the rope in her hand, hoping that
'how much' and 'I'll buy' would be sufficient to
make them agree, for the life of her she couldn't
think of anything else to say to the point. Yes, one
more word. She ordered briskly '*Kom*' and had the
satisfaction of seeing them bunch together round the
cart once more, obviously waiting for her to lead the
way.

She didn't know anything about donkeys, and she
prayed that this one would answer to the gentle tug
she gave its worn bridle. It did, and she made her way
to the front, not hurrying because the donkey's hooves
were in a frightful state. It took longer to go back too,
because she thought the tinkers might be more im-
pressed if she went in through the main gates, and
every yard of the way she was hiding panic that they
might come to their senses and make off with the donkey before she could reach home. But the gates were
reached at last and she singled out the scruffy man,
beckoning him to follow her, leaving the rest of them
grouped in the drive staring at them. The man began
to mutter to himself before they reached the sweep before the house, but Caroline didn't listen. She was
planning what she would do; open the door and shout
for Noakes to mind the donkey and keep an eye on the
man while she fetched some money—and that was another problem; how much did one pay for a worn out
starving animal? Perhaps Noakes would know.

The Professor, home early for his lunch and thus breaking a rule he had adhered to for years without knowing quite why, was standing at the drawing-room windows, staring out over the grounds, aware of disappointment because Caro wasn't home. He frowned at the dripping landscape before him and then frowned again, staring even harder. Unless his splendid eyesight deceived him, his wife, a most disreputable man and a very battered donkey were coming up his drive, and what was more, there were people clustered round the gates, peering in. Something about the small resolute figure marching up to the front door sent him striding to open it and down the steps to meet her.

Caro, almost at the door and seeing her husband's vast form coming down the steps with deliberate speed, felt a wave of relief so strong that she could have burst into tears. She swallowed them back and cried: 'Oh, Radinck, I'm so glad you're home!' She had to raise her voice because he was barely within earshot. 'I've bought this poor little donkey, but I don't know how much to pay the man—I got him to come with me while I fetched the money. I thought Noakes would know, but now you're here you can tell me.' She looked up at him with complete confidence and added, just in case he didn't realise the urgency of the occasion: 'She's a jenny and she's going to foal soon; they were beating her, and just look at her hooves!'

The Professor looked, running a gentle hand over the bruised back, bending to examine each wretched neglected hoof, then he straightened up to tower over the tinker.

Caro couldn't understand a word he was saying. His voice was quiet and unhurried, but the tinker looked at first cowed and then downright scared. Finally, the Professor produced his notecase, selected what he wanted from its contents and handed them to the man, who grabbed them and, looking considerably shaken, made off as fast as his legs would carry him.

Caro watched him join his family at the gates and disappear. 'That was splendid of you, Radinck,' she said in deep satisfaction. 'I couldn't understand what you said, of course, but you scared him, didn't you? Oh, I'm so very glad you were here... I'll pay you back in a minute, but I ought to see to this poor thing first. What did you say to that horrid man?'

Her husband looked down at her, a half smile twitching his mouth. 'Enough to make him very careful how he treats any more animals he may own in future, and allow me to give her to you as a gift.' The half smile became a real one and she smiled back at him in delight. 'Tell me, how did you get him to come here?'

She told him and he laughed, a bellow of genuine amusement which set her hopeful heart racing,

although all she said was, 'We ought to get in out of
this rain. Where shall I take her?' And before he
could answer: 'There's that barn next to the stables
where the hay's kept…'

He gave her a questioning look. 'I didn't know
you were interested in the stables—yes, the barn
would do very well.'

Caroline began to lead the animal towards the
back of the house. 'I'm not sure what donkeys eat.
I'll ask Jan—he'll get me some carrots, though.'

Radinck gave her an amused glance. 'Jan too?' he
asked, and then: 'She can go into the south field with
the horses once she's rested.'

They were halfway there when Caro asked: 'What
did you mean—"Jan too"?'

He answered her carelessly: 'Oh, you seem to
have a way with people, don't you? The servants fall
over themselves to please you and now Jan, who
never does anything for anyone unless he wants to.'

'He's a dear old man,' declared Caro warmly, re-
membering Jan's deep elderly voice rumbling out the
carols of an evening. 'He had a frightful cold, you
know—I told him what to do for it.' She glanced
sideways at him. 'I hope you don't mind?'

He sounded irritable. 'I don't suppose it would
make any difference whether I minded or not. Give
me that rope, and be good enough to go up to the
house and ask Noakes to get Jan and young Willem,

then telephone the vet and tell him to come out as soon as he can to examine an ill-treated donkey in foal.'

'Yes, of course.' Caroline smiled happily at his rather irritable face. 'I'll go at once. Radinck, what shall we call her?'

He was staring at her with hard eyes as though he couldn't bear the sight of her. 'What could be more appropriate than Caro?' he wanted to know mockingly.

She hadn't taken a dozen steps before he was beside her, his hands on her shoulders so that she had to stop.

'I'm sorry, that was a rotten thing to say.'

She had gone a little white and the tears were thick in her throat, but she managed a smile. 'As a matter of fact it's a very good name for her.' She added earnestly: 'It doesn't matter, really it doesn't.'

'It does—you didn't deserve it, Caroline.' His voice was gentle. 'What shall we call her? We have a Waterloo and a Rex and the kitchen cat is called Anja—how about Queenie, and if the foal is a boy we can call him Prince.'

Caro had no doubt that he was trying to placate her hurt feelings, and although it wasn't much the tiny flame of hope she kept flickering deep down inside her brightened a little; at least he had realised that he had hurt her. She smiled at him a bit crookedly. 'That's a splendid name,' she agreed. 'I'll get Noakes.'

She slipped away before he could say anything else and took care not to return until she saw Jan and Willem going towards the stables.

Radinck had fetched a bucket of water and some oats while she had been gone and now the three men stood watching the donkey making a meal. She was still happily munching when Mijnheer Stagsma arrived. Radinck explained briefly what had happened, introduced Caro and waited patiently while the vet wished her happiness in her marriage, congratulated her on her rescue of the donkey, hoped that his wife would have the pleasure of calling on her soon and enquired how she liked her new home.

He was a youngish man with a friendly face. Caro would have enjoyed talking to him, but out of the corner of her eye she saw her husband's bland face watching them. He was growing impatient, so she brought their cheerful little talk to a friendly end and indicated the patient.

Mijnheer Stagsma took a long time, muttering to himself and occasionally saying something to the Professor. At length he came upright again.

'Nothing serious, I think—starved, of course, but that can be dealt with, and I'll deal with those hooves as soon as she's stronger. I should think she'll have the foal in a week or so—it's hard to tell in her present state. I'll give her a couple of injections and some

ointment for those sores on her back. Who'll be looking after her?'

Caro, striving to understand what he said, looked
at Radinck. He answered the vet, spoke to Willem
who grinned and nodded and then turned to Caro,
telling her what the vet had said.

'Oh, good—Willem doesn't mind feeding her? I
don't…'

'No, not you, Caroline. You may visit her, of
course, and take her out when she is better, but
Willem will tend her and clean out the barn.'

She supposed that being a baroness barred her
from such chores. 'If you say so,' she said happily,
'but I simply must learn Dutch as quickly as possible.'

The glimmer of a smile touched her husband's
face. 'You seem to manage very well—but I'll arrange for you to have lessons.'

They wished the vet goodbye, standing together
on the sweep as he drove down the drive and out of
sight.

'Oh, dear—should I have asked him in for a
drink?' asked Caro.

'I already did so, but he couldn't stop—he's a
very busy man.'

'And nice—so friendly.' She didn't see the look
her husband shot at her. 'May I go back and look at
Queenie?'

He turned away to go into the house. 'There is no need to ask my permission, Caroline. I am not your gaoler—you are free to do exactly what you like as long as you don't interfere with my work.'

'Not your work,' said Caro, suddenly passionate, 'your life—and never fear, Radinck, I'll take care never to do that.'

She marched away, her chin in the air, in one of her rare tempers.

But her tempers didn't last long. Within half an hour they were lunching together and although she didn't apologise for her outburst she tried to be friendly. She supposed that it was for Noakes' benefit that Radinck met her conversational efforts more than halfway. It was a disappointment when he told her that he wouldn't be home for dinner. She spent her afternoon wrestling with an ever-lengthening list of Dutch words and the evening coaching her choir once again, and before she went to bed she went down to the stables to take a look at Queenie. The little donkey looked better already, she thought. She pulled the ragged ears gently, offered a carrot and went back to the house, where she mooned around for another hour or so before going to bed much later than usual, hoping that Radinck would come back before she did. But there was no sign of him. She fell asleep at last and didn't hear him return in the small hours of the morning.

She was up early and with Waterloo in attendance went down to see how Queenie had fared. Willem was already there, cleaning out the barn and feeding her, and Caro, trying out some of her carefully acquired Dutch, made out that the donkey had improved considerably, but Willem was busy and she didn't like to hinder him, so she wandered off again into the crisp morning—just right for a ride, she decided, and with Waterloo trotting beside her, hurried back for breakfast.

Jan was waiting for her when she got to the stables and Jemmy greeted her with a toss of the head and a playful nip. Caroline mounted his plump back and walked him out of the yard and into the field beyond. Walk round once, Jan had told her, then trot round once. She did so, watched by the old man, and then because she was feeling confident and enjoying herself she poked Jemmy's fat sides with her heels and started off again. Jemmy was enjoying himself too; his trot broke into a canter and Caro, her hair flying, let out a whoopee of delight. They were three quarters of the way round the field when she saw Radinck standing beside Jan.

CHAPTER SIX

THERE WAS ONLY one thing to do and that was to go on. Caroline finished circling the field and pulled up untidily in front of Radinck. Jan was standing beside him, but she couldn't tell from the craggy old face if anything had been said. To be on the safe side she leaned down from her saddle. 'Don't you dare be angry with Jan!' she hissed fiercely. 'I made him teach me—he thought I was doing it as a lovely surprise for you.'

'And were you?' It was impossible to tell if Radinck was angry or not.

'Well, yes—but not just for you. I thought that as you're a baron and have a lot of posh friends you might be ashamed of me if I couldn't do all the things they do...'

The gleam in Radinck's eyes became very pronounced, but he answered gravely: 'That was very thoughtful of you, Caroline. Were you going to use it as an argument in favour of inviting my—er—posh friends here?'

He was impossible! She looked away from him at the gentle countryside around them. 'No,' she said evenly, 'I promised that I wouldn't interfere with your life, didn't I? You seem to have forgotten that. It was only that I didn't want to let you down.'

'I beg your pardon, you are...' He stopped and started again. 'I should enjoy your company each morning before breakfast.'

'Would you really?' Her eyes searched his face. 'I saw you the first morning we were here, you know, that's when I made up my mind to learn to ride. But I'm not very good, it was lucky I didn't fall off just now.'

'Jan has taught you very well.' Radinck turned and spoke to the old man, who grinned at him and answered at some length, and then turned back to her. 'Jan says that all you need now is practice. It is a pity that I have an appointment this morning, otherwise I would have ridden with you.' His gaze swept over her. 'But I think you must have the right clothes. I'm free after lunch until the early evening. I'll take you into Leeuwarden and get you kitted up.'

Caro stammered a little. 'Oh, that would be s-super, but isn't it taking up your time? If you tell me where to go, I c-could go on my own.'

'We'll go together, Caroline,' and just as she was

relishing this he added briskly: 'You would have no idea what to get, in the first place, and the shop is extremely hard to find.'

He was right about the shop; it was tucked away in a narrow street lined with old gabled houses, squeezed between a shirtmakers and a gentleman's hatters. Following Radinck inside, Caro wondered where on earth the customers went, and then discovered that the narrow little shop went back and back, one room opening into the next. The owner of the shop knew Radinck; he was ushered into a small room at the back, its walls lined with shelves stacked with cloth and boxes of riding boots and beautifully folded jodhpurs. Here he was given a chair while Caro was whisked into a still smaller room where, with an elderly lady to observe the conventions, she was fitted with boots, several white sweaters and shirts, a riding hat, a crop and a pair of jodhpurs, and finally the jacket. Looking at herself in the mirror she hardly recognised her image. 'Oh, very elegant,' she said out loud, and, obedient to the old tailor's beckoning finger, went rather shyly to show herself to Radinck. She stood quietly while he looked her over.

'Very nice, Caroline,' and then, to her surprise: 'What size are you?'

'In England I'm a size ten, I don't know what I am in Holland.' She was on the point of asking him why he wanted to know and then thought better of it; instead she said, 'Thank you very much, Rad-inck.'

He gave her a half smile. 'What else can you do, Caroline?'

She gave him a surprised look. 'Me? Well, noth-ing really—I can swim, but only just, if you know what I mean, and I can play the piano a bit and dance a bit...'

'You drive a car?'

She shook her head. 'No—I've never needed to, you see.'

'You shall have lessons and later on a car of your own. Tennis?'

'Well, yes.' She added waspishly: 'I hope I've passed.'

He turned away from her. 'You would have done that even if you could do none of these things. If you're quite satisfied with the things we'll get them packed up and I'll drive you back.'

She had deserved the snub, she supposed. She wondered for the hundredth time why Radinck had married her; she hadn't been a very good bargain.

Fairmindedness made her stop there; he had wanted a sheet anchor and she had said that she would be one. She belonged in the background of his life, always there when he wanted her, and it would be a good thing if she remembered that more often.

On the way back she did her best. 'I expect,' she

said carefully, 'that now you've had time to think about it, you'd rather I didn't ride with you in the mornings—it's something you hadn't reckoned on, isn't it? And that wasn't why I wanted to learn to ride,' she finished with a rush.

He had turned off the motorway and had slowed the pace a little, because the road was narrow. 'I didn't think it was; shall we try it out for a day or two and see what happens?'

Caroline agreed quietly and just as quietly wished him goodbye presently. He had already told her that he had an appointment and she forbore from asking him if he would be home for dinner. She was surprised when he told her that he would see her about seven o'clock.

She wore one of the new dresses, a silk jersey in old rose with a demure stand-up collar and long sleeves, and when he got back she was sitting by the fire in the drawing-room engrossed in some tapestry work she had bought as an alternative to the sweater. She wished him a demure good evening and set a group of stitches with care. There was a pleasantly excited glow under the new dress, for Radinck had paused in the doorway and was looking at her in a way he had never looked at her before. The stitches went all wrong, but this was no time to look anything but serene and casual. She went on stitching, the needle going in and out, just as though she knew what she was doing; there would be a lot of unpicking to do later. Radinck advanced into the room, offered her a drink and went to fetch it from the sofa table under the window. As he handed it to her he observed, with the air of a man trying out words he had almost forgotten: 'You look pretty, Caroline.'

The glow rushed to her cheeks, but she answered composedly: 'Thank you—this is one of my new dresses, it is charming, isn't it?'

'I was referring to you, Caroline.'

'Oh, how kind.' That sounded silly, so she added: 'The right clothes make such a difference, you know.'

She bent to scratch Rex's woolly ear and then offered the same service to Waterloo, sitting beside the dog. 'I went to see Queenie this evening,' she told him. 'It's a wonder how she's picked up, and Willem's done wonders with her coat already.'

'I've just come from there—she's reacting very nicely to the antibiotic.' Radinck sat down in the great winged chair opposite her, his long legs stretched out, his glass in his hand, and when she looked up briefly it was to find him staring at her again, his eyes very bright. It seemed a good idea to apply herself to her tapestry and by the time Noakes came to announce dinner was ready she had made a fine mess of it.

And to her surprised delight, after dinner, instead of going to his study or out again, Radinck followed her into the drawing-room and sat drinking his coffee, giving no sign of wanting to go anywhere else. Her fingers shook as she fell upon the tapestry once again, but her face was quiet enough as she gave him a quick peep. He had stretched himself out comfortably and was reading a newspaper—perhaps he had forgotten that she was there.

But he hadn't, and presently he began to talk; observations on the news, describing an interesting case he had had at the hospital that day and going on to ask her if she would like to start Dutch lessons straight away as he had found someone suitable to teach her.

She replied suitably to everything he said and presently, loath to do so, for she could have sat there for ever with him, she declared her intention of going to bed; it would never do for him to discover that she was eager for his company. She gave him a quiet goodnight and went to the door, aware as she went through it that he was looking at her again. She was halfway along the gallery above the hall when he called to her, and she stopped and leaned over the balustrade to ask 'Yes, Radinck?'

'You have forgotten that we are to ride together in the morning?'

'No, Radinck. Shall I meet you at the stables?'

'No, I shall be here at half past seven.' He said goodnight again as she turned away.

Contrary to her expectations Caroline slept dreamlessly until she was wakened by Ilke with her morning tea. She drank it while she dressed, afraid of being late. Actually she raced downstairs with a couple of minutes to spare, to find Radinck waiting for her. She thought he looked splendid in his riding kit and longed to tell him so. He wished her good morning and without wasting time they went to the stables. It was almost light with a clear sky and a cold wind and the grass was touched with frost. 'If it gets much colder you will have to stop riding—once the ground gets too hard there's more chance of a toss.'

She said, 'Yes, Radinck,' meekly. Frost or no frost, she would go on riding as long as he did.

The stables were lighted and Willem was there, busy with Jemmy and Rufus, Radinck's great bay horse. Caro, her fingers crossed, contrived to mount neatly and watched while Radinck swung himself into the saddle, whistled to Rex, and led the way out of the yard. He hadn't fussed over her at all, merely wanted to know if she were ready and carelessly told her to straighten her back. 'We'll go over the fields as far as the lane and go round the outside of the wall,' he told her. 'Don't trot Jemmy in the fields, but you may do so in the lane.'

Caro, completely overshadowed by man and

horse, craned her neck to answer him. 'Yes, very well, but I expect you like a gallop, don't you?'

'Yes, I do—but not this morning. I must find a quiet little mare for you and then we can gallop together—it hardly seems fair to expect Jemmy to do more than trot.'

She patted the pony's neck. 'He's a darling— wouldn't he mind if I rode another horse?'

Radinck laughed. 'He's been here for years— he's quite elderly now, he'll be good company for Queenie and her foal.'

They reached the first field and once out of it started to trot, and presently when they reached the gate to the lane beyond Radinck said: 'Now try a canter, Caroline.'

She acquitted herself very well, although by the time they got back she was shaking with nerves, terrified that she would fall off or do something stupid, but she didn't, and had the pleasure of hearing her husband say as they went indoors: 'That went very well—do you care to ride each morning while the weather's fine?'

She tried not to sound eager. 'Oh, please, if you'd like to.'

He turned to give her a suddenly cool look. 'I should hardly have asked you if I hadn't wanted to, Caroline. Shall we have breakfast in fifteen minutes?'

'Yes, I'll tell Juffrouw Kropp.' She went along the passage to the kitchen, gave her message and went upstairs to shower and change, her feelings mixed. Radinck had seemed so friendly, then suddenly he had drawn back and looked at her as though he didn't like her after all. She was in two minds not to go down to breakfast, but if she didn't he might think that she minded being snubbed... She changed into a tweed skirt and sweater, tied her hair back and went to join him.

He was already at the table when she got downstairs, but he got up to draw out her chair, handed her her letters, and went back to reading his own. It was to be a silent meal, she guessed; for the time being she wasn't a sheet anchor at all, only a nuisance. She murmured a cheerful good morning to Noakes when he came with fresh coffee, and immersed herself in her post—a letter from Clare, excitedly telling her the news that she was engaged, one from her aunt, asking vaguely if she were happy and regretting that she hadn't been able to attend the wedding, and a card from Sister Pringle inviting her to her wedding in the New Year. Caroline was wondering what to do about it when Radinck leaned across and handed her a pile of opened letters. 'Invitations,' he told her. 'Will you answer them?'

She glanced through them and counted six and looked up in surprise. 'But Radinck, how strange! I mean, we've been here for almost two weeks and no one has even telephoned, and now all these on the same day.'

His smile mocked her. 'My dear girl, have you forgotten that we are supposed to be newlyweds? It would hardly have been decent to have called on us or invited us anywhere for at least a fortnight.' He tossed a letter across the table to her. 'Here's a letter from Rebecca—Tiele's wife. She wants us to go over for drinks soon—she will ring you some time today.'

'Am I to accept?'

He looked faintly surprised. 'Of course. Tiele is a close friend, and I hope you and Rebecca will be friends too. As for the others, if I tell Anna to type out the correct answer in Dutch perhaps you would copy it and get them sent off.'

Caroline glanced through them; three invitations to drinks, one to the burgermeester's reception in Leeuwarden and two for evening parties.

'But, Radinck—' she began, and stopped so he looked up rather impatiently.

'Well?'

'You don't like going out,' she observed, not mincing her words. 'You said so—you like peace and quiet and time to read and…'

'You do not need to remind me, my dear Caroline, I am aware of what I like. However, there are certain conventions which must be observed. We will accept the invitations we receive, and at Christmas I will— I beg your pardon—we will give a large party. By then you will have met everyone who is acquainted with me and we can revert to a normal life here. You will have had the opportunity of making any friends you wish and doubtless you will find life sufficiently entertaining.'

Words bubbled and boiled on Caro's tongue, and she went quite red in the face choking them back. The awful thought that she was fighting a losing battle assailed her, but not for long; she had had a glimpse just once or twice of Radinck's other self hidden away behind all that ill humour. She told herself that it needed patience and all the love she had for him, and she had plenty of both.

Rebecca telephoned later that morning and Caro liked her voice immediately. 'We're not far from you,' said Rebecca, 'and I've been dying to come and see you, but Tiele said you were entitled to a couple of weeks' peace and quiet together. Will you come over for drinks? Could Radinck manage tomorrow evening, do you think—I'm going to invite you to dinner too, but if he's got something on, ring me back, will you, and we'll be content with drinks. Have you settled down?'

'Yes, thank you, though I wish I could speak Dutch, but everyone's so kind.'

'Radinck told Tiele that you were managing very well—have you started lessons yet?'

'No, but Radinck said he'd found someone to teach me.'

Rebecca giggled. 'Well, you've not had much time to bother about lessons, have you?'

She rang off presently and Caro went to her room and looked through her wardrobe, wondering what she should wear. She came to the perfectly normal female conclusion that she hadn't anything, and then changed her mind. The rose pink jersey would do; it had had a good effect the other evening, and after all, it was Radinck she wanted to notice her, not Tiele and Rebecca.

She broached the subject of going to dinner when Radinck came home for lunch and managed not to show her disappointment when he said that it was quite impossible. He had a hospital governors' meeting to attend at eight o'clock; he would drive her back from the Raukema van den Ecks and go straight on to the hospital where he would get a meal later. He looked at her sharply as he said it, but she met the look calmly, remarking that it would be nice to meet another English girl. 'She sounded sweet,' she declared. 'Would you like your coffee here or in the drawing-room?'

'I'm due back in ten minutes—I won't wait. Don't wait dinner for me either, Caroline; I'll have some sandwiches when I get back.' He was at the door when he paused and asked: 'Will you come riding tomorrow morning?'

'Well, yes, I should like to. The same time?'

He nodded as he went out of the room.

Caroline didn't see him for the rest of that day, but he was waiting for her when she went downstairs the next morning. The weather was being kind, cold and windy but dry, and the skies were clear. She acquitted herself very well, although Radinck had very little to say as they rode across the fields and after a few remarks about Queenie and a request that she should be ready that evening by half past six he fell silent. It was when they had returned to the house and were crossing the hall that he observed that he would be unable to get home for lunch. He spoke in his usual austere way, but she thought that she detected regret and her spirits rose.

They stayed that way too. The morning filled with her visit to see Marta, a solemn consultation with Juffrouw Kropp about the renewal of some kitchen equipment, a visit to Queenie, now looking almost plump, and an hour at the piano. And the afternoon went quickly too. By half past five Caroline was upstairs in her room trying out different hairstyles and making up her face. In the end she toned down the make-up and decided to keep to her usual hairstyle, partly because she was afraid that if she attempted anything else it would disintegrate halfway through the evening. The pink jersey dress was entirely satisfactory, though. She gave a final long look in the pier glass, and went down to the sitting-room.

It wasn't quite half past six and she hadn't expected Radinck to be waiting for her, but he was, in an elegant dark suit, looking as though he hadn't just done a day's work at the hospital, only sat about in idleness. Caroline wondered how he did it. He allowed himself very little recreation. One day, she thought with real terror, he would have a coronary...

He got up as she went in, took her coat from her and held it while she got into it and they went out together. Beyond greeting her he had said nothing and nor had she, but once on the sweep she was surprised into exclaiming: 'But where's the Aston Martin?'

There was another car standing there and she went closer to see what it was. A Panther de Ville; she had only seen one or two before. Now she admired the elegance and choked over its price. She hadn't quite believed Radinck when he had said that he was rich, now she decided that she had been mistaken. Only someone with a great deal of money could afford to buy, let alone run such a motor car. 'What a lovely car,' she said faintly. 'Is it yours?'

'Yes.' He opened the door and she got in, cudgelling her brains to find some way of making him say more than yes or no. She was still worrying about it as he drove off and since he had very little to say during the brief journey, she had time to worry some more. Perhaps it was a good thing when they arrived and she had to empty her head of worries and respond to the friendly welcome from Tiele and his wife.

Rebecca, Caro was relieved to see, wasn't pretty; beautifully made up, exquisitely dressed, but not pretty, although it was apparent at once that her husband considered her the most beautiful woman in the world.

They took to each other at once and Caro was borne away to see the new baby before they had drinks. 'A darling,' declared Caro, and meant it.

'Yes, he is,' agreed his doting mother, 'but he keeps us busy, I can tell you, although we've got a marvellous nanny.' She giggled enchantingly. 'The poor dear doesn't get a look in!' She tucked an arm into Caro's as they went down the stairs. 'Tiele's a splendid father—he's a nice husband too. Radinck's a dear, isn't he? And that's a silly question!' They had reached the drawing-room and she laughingly repeated her remark to the men. 'As though Caro's going to admit anything!' she declared. Caro was glad to see that Radinck laughed too, although he didn't look at her, which was a good thing because she had got rather pink in the face.

There seemed to be a great deal to talk about and she found herself listening to Radinck's voice, warm and friendly, teasing Becky, exchanging views with Tiele, including her punctiliously in the talk so that they gave what she hoped was a splendid impression of a happily married couple. She was sorry to leave, but since they were to see each other again at the burgermeester's reception, she was able to echo her husband's '*Tot ziens*' cheerfully enough. But he showed no inclination to discuss their evening, indeed he didn't speak until they were almost halfway home.

'You enjoyed your evening?' he asked her. 'You liked Becky?'

'Very much; she's sweet, and such a darling little baby.'

Her husband grunted and she wished she hadn't said that; she hurried on to cover the little silence: 'It's nice that we shall see each other at the reception.'

'Yes. You will also meet a number of my friends there. You answered the invitations?'

'Yes, and three more came with the afternoon post.'

'Will you leave them on the hall table? I'll make sure they're friends and not just acquaintances.'

'You're not coming in before you go—wherever you're going?'

'I have no time.' She couldn't help but notice how

cold his voice had become. She sighed very softly and didn't speak again until they reached the house, when she said hurriedly: 'No, don't get out, Radinck, I'm sure you're pressed for time.'

She jumped out of the car and ran up the steps where the watchful Noakes was already standing by the open door. 'We'll ride in the morning?' Radinck called after her. Caroline had been afraid he wasn't going to say that, so, careful not to sound eager, she said over her shoulder: 'I'll see you then,' and ran indoors.

She saw him much sooner than that, though. Left alone, she had whipped down to the stables to see how Queenie was, gone round the outside of the house with Rex, who was feeling hurt because Radinck had gone without him, had her dinner, conducted her choir and then gone upstairs to bed. She had been there two hours or more sitting up against her pillows reviewing her evening when she heard Queenie's voice—not loud, not nearly loud enough to rouse everyone else in the house, with their rooms right on the other side. Nor would Willem hear her, living as he did in a small cottage on the estate boundary with his mother. The noise came again and Caro got out of bed, put on her quilted dressing gown, whipped a pair of boots from the closet, and crept through the house. Radinck wasn't in and she had no idea when he would return. She could take a look at Queenie and if things weren't going right, she could get a message to Willem or old Jan, who would know what to do, and if necessary she could get Mijnheer Stagsma.

She let herself out of the side door nearest the stables, into the very cold, clear night, and, glad of her boots but wishing she had put on something thicker than a dressing gown, made her way to the yard. There was a light in the barn. She switched it on and went to peer at the donkey. Queenie looked back at her with gentle eyes. She was lying down on her bed of straw and even to Caro, who didn't know much about it, it was obvious that she was about to produce her foal. But whether she was in need of help was another thing. She might have been calling for company; after all, it was a lonely business, giving birth.

Caro knelt down by Queenie's head and rubbed the long furry ears; for the moment she wasn't sure what to do. 'I'll wait just for a few minutes,' she told Queenie, 'and if something doesn't start to happen by then I'll go and get help. It's a pity that Radinck isn't here, but even if he were, I wouldn't like to bother him. You see, Queenie, he doesn't…' Her soft voice spiralled into a small shriek as her husband spoke from the dimness of the door.

'I saw the light—it's Queenie, isn't it?' He came and stood beside the pair of them, and it was difficult to see his face clearly. Caroline nodded, her heart still thumping with fright, and he took off his car coat and his jacket, rolled up his shirt sleeves and knelt down to take a closer look at the donkey. 'Any minute now,' he pronounced. 'Everything looks fine. How long have you been here?'

'Ten minutes, perhaps a little longer.'

'Did she wake you up?'

She answered without much thought. 'No—I hadn't been to sleep.'

He had his head bent. 'It's almost two o'clock.' He turned to look at her then, a slow look taking in her tousled hair and the dressing gown. 'My dear good girl, it's winter! You should have put on something warmer than that.'

'I am wearing my boots,' Caro declared as though that was a sufficient answer, and added: 'I didn't want to waste time in case Queenie was ill.'

'And what did you intend to do?' he wanted to know.

'Well, I said I'd wait just a few minutes and then if she went on groaning and looking distressed I thought I'd go and get Jan up—only he's old, I didn't want to bother him.'

He put a gentle hand on the beast's heaving flanks. 'You didn't want to bother me either, Caroline.' His voice was quiet.

'No.' For something to do she ran her fingers through her untidy hair.

'Leave your hair.' He still spoke quietly and she dropped her hands in astonishment. After a moment he said: 'Look!'

The foal was enchanting. 'We shall be able to call him Prince,' observed Radinck as they watched him get to his wobbly legs and nuzzle his mother. 'Caroline, do you think you could make some hot mash? Willem should have it ready for the morning over in the far corner. There's a Primus—just warm it up, Queenie could do with it now. I'll stay here for a minute or two just to make sure everything's as it should be.'

Caroline went obediently, found the mash and the stove and waited while it heated, and presently went back with it to find that Radinck had fetched a bucket of water which Queenie was drinking thirstily. She gobbled down the mash too, standing between the pair of them. She was still far from being in the pink of condition, but she was clean and combed and content. Caro, sitting back on her heels so that she could see more of the foal, observed: 'Oh, isn't it lovely? She's so happy.' She caught her breath. 'What would have happened to her if we hadn't taken her in?'

'Oh, she would have been left in a field to fend for herself.' Radinck didn't add to that because Caro's eyes were filled with tears.

'In a couple of days she shall go out into the fields with the horses. She's almost strong enough—they like company, you know, and horses like them.'

Queenie finished her meal, arranged herself comfortably on the straw with the foal beside her and wagged her ears. 'She's telling us we can go,' said Radinck. 'She'll do very well until Willem comes.' He pulled Caro to her feet, draped his jacket round her and walked her back through the moonlight night to the side door. Inside she would have gone to bed, but he kept an arm round her shoulders. 'I have a fancy for a cup of tea,' he declared. 'Let's go to the kitchen and make one—it will warm you, too.'

He seemed to know where everything was. Caro, her arms in the sleeves of his jacket to make things a little easier, got mugs, sugar and milk while he fetched a teapot and a tea canister, found a loaf and some butter and put them on the table. 'Didn't you have any dinner?' asked Caro.

'Yes—only it was a very dainty one. I have been famished for the last hour.'

'Oh, that's a terrible feeling,' agreed Caro, 'and one always thinks of all the nicest things to eat. I've often...' She stopped herself just in time. He wouldn't want to know that she had sometimes been rather hungry; hospital meals cost money and although one could eat adequately enough if one were careful, there was never anything left over for chocolate clairs and steak and sole bonne femme.

'Well?' asked Radinck.

'Nothing.' She busied herself pouring the tea

while he sliced bread and spread it lavishly with butter.

Caroline hadn't enjoyed a meal as much for a long time. It was as though Radinck was a different person. She wasn't just having a glimpse of him as he really was, he was letting her get to know him. She found herself talking to him as though she had known him all her life. She had forgotten to worry that he might, at any moment, revert to his normal severe manner. Everything was wonderful. She sat there, eating slices of bread and butter, oblivious of her tatty appearance, talking about Queenie, and her riding and how she was going to learn to speak Dutch and what fun it was to have found a friend in Becky. And Radinck did nothing to stop her—indeed, he encouraged her with cleverly put questions which she answered with all the spontaneous simplicity of a small girl. It was the old-fashioned wall clock striking a ponderous three which brought her up short. She began to collect up the mugs and plates, stammering a little. 'I'm sorry—I've kept you out of bed, I don't know what came over me.'

He took the things from her and put them back on the table. 'Leave those. Will you be too tired to ride in the morning?'

'Tired? Heavens, no, I wouldn't miss…' She stopped herself again. 'The mornings are lovely at this time of year,' she observed rather woodenly.

Radinck was staring down at her. 'I must agree with you, Caroline—the mornings are lovely.' He turned away abruptly and went over to the sink with the teapot and she watched him, idly sticking her hands into the pockets of his jacket which she still wore draped round her. There was something in one of them. She just had time to pull it almost out to look at it before he turned round; she only had a glimpse, but it was enough. It was a handkerchief—a woman's handkerchief, new but crumpled.

They walked out of the kitchen together and up the stairs, and all the way Caroline told herself that she had no reason to mind so much. She had taken her hands out of the pockets as though they were full of hot coals and handed him his jacket with a murmur of thanks, aware of a pain almost physical. If she was going to feel like this every time she encountered some small sign that she wasn't the only woman in his life, then she might just as well give up at once. Of course, the handkerchief could belong to an aunt or a cousin or…he had no relations living close by. It could belong, said a nasty little voice at the back of her head, to whoever it was he went to see almost every evening in the week. Then why had he married her? Couldn't the handkerchief's owner have been a sheet anchor too? She thought of herself as a shabby, reliable coat, always at hand hanging on the back door, necessary but never worn anywhere but in the back yard in bad weather, whereas a really smart coat would be taken from the closet with care and pride and displayed to one's friends.

At the top of the stairs she wished him goodnight and was quite unprepared for his sudden swoop and his hard, quick kiss. She turned without a word and fled into her room, aware that any other girl with her wits about her would have known how to deal with the situation.

CHAPTER SEVEN

IF CARO HADN'T BEEN so sleepy she might have lain awake and pondered Radinck's behaviour, but beyond a fleeting sense of elation mixed with a good deal of puzzlement, there was no time to think at all; she was asleep as her head touched the pillow. And in the morning there was no time for anything but getting dressed by half past seven. As she went downstairs she did wonder if she would feel awkward when she saw him, but that need not have worried her. He offered her a cool good morning, led her down to the stables, watched her mount, had a word with Willem about Queenie, and led the way into the fields. They rode in almost complete silence and on their return, even the sight of Queenie and her foal called forth no more than a further businesslike discussion with Willem as to their welfare. They were back to square one, thought Caro. Last night had been an episode to be forgotten or at least ignored.

She remembered the hanky with a pang of sheer envy, subdued it with difficulty and loitered to add her own remarks to Willem, who, with the rest of the staff at Huis Thoe, made a point of understanding her peculiar Dutch.

By the time she got down to breakfast, Radinck was almost ready to leave. Caroline wasn't in the least surprised when he mentioned that he wouldn't be home for lunch. She was glad that there was so much to keep her occupied. It wasn't until after lunch that the wicked little thought that she might take another look at the handkerchief in Radinck's jacket pocket entered her head. The suit was to be sent to the cleaners, along with her dressing gown; they would be in one of the small rooms leading from the passage which led to the kitchen.

They were there all right. Feeling guilty, she searched every pocket and found the handkerchief gone. It must be something very precious to Radinck and it served her right for snooping. Feeling ashamed of herself, she put on her sheepskin jacket, pulled a woollen cap over her head and went to find Rex, prowling in discontent from room to room. He had been left behind again. They went a long way, indeed they were still only halfway home in the gathering dusk when Radinck opened his house door. He had a large box under one arm and went at once to the sitting-room where Caro liked to spend her leisure.

The room was empty of course, and in answer to his summons, Noakes informed him that the Baroness had gone out with Rex. 'Been gorn a long time, too,' observed Noakes. 'Great walker, she is too.' He turned to go, adding with a trusted old friend's freedom: 'Walking away from somethin', if yer ask me.'

His employer turned cold blue eyes on him. 'And what exactly does that mean?'

Noakes threw him a quick shrewd look. 'Just me opinion, Professor, take it or leave it, as you might say.'

'She's unhappy? The Baroness is unhappy?'

'Not ter say unhappy—always busy, she is, with this and that—flowers in the rooms and ordering stores and learning Dutch all by 'erself. 'Omesick, I've no doubt, Professor.' He added defiantly: 'She's on 'er own a lot.'

The master of the house looked coldly furious. 'I have my work, Noakes.'

'And now, beggin' yer pardon, Professor, you've got 'er as well.'

The Professor looked like a thundercloud. 'It is a good thing that we are old friends, Noakes…'

His faithful butler had a prudent hand on the door. 'Yes, Professor—I'd not 'ave said any of that if we 'adn't been.'

The austere lines of the Professor's face broke into a smile. 'I know that, Noakes, and I value your friendship.'

Caro walked in half an hour later, her cheeks glowing, her hair regrettably untidy. As she came into the hall from the garden door, Rex beside her, she saw Noakes on his stately way to the kitchen.

'Noakes!' she cried. 'We've had a lovely walk, I'm as warm as toast. And don't frown at me, I've wiped Rex's feet. I went to see Queenie too and she's fine.' She had thrown off her jacket and was pulling the cap off her head when the sitting-room door opened and she saw Radinck.

Her breath left her, as it always did when she saw him. After a little silence she said: 'Hullo, Radinck, I didn't know you'd be home early. I hope you've had tea—we went further than we meant to.'

He leaned against the wall, his bland face giving nothing away. 'I waited for you, Caroline.' He nodded at Noakes who hurried kitchenwards and held the door wide for her to go in. The room looked very welcoming; the fire burned brightly in the grate and Waterloo had made himself comfortable before it, joined, after he had made much of his master, by Rex. Caro sat down on the little armchair by the work table she had made her own, smoothed her hair without bothering much about it, and picked up her tapestry work. She had painstakingly unpicked it and now had the miserable task of working it again. She smiled across at her husband. 'I hope it's scones, I've been showing Marta how to make them.'

He said gravely: 'I look forward to them. Caroline, are you lonely?'

The question was so unexpected that she pricked her finger. She said rather loudly: 'Lonely? Why, of course not—there's so much to do, and now I'm going to start Dutch lessons, tomorrow, and Juffrouw Kropp is teaching me how to be a good housekeeper, and there are the animals...' She paused, seeking something to add to her meagre list of activities. 'Oh, and now there's Becky...'

Noakes brought in the tea tray then and she busied herself pouring it from the George the Second silver bullet teapot into the delicate cups. It wasn't being rich that mattered, she mused, it was possessing beautiful things, lovingly made and treasured and yet used each day...

'Queenie and Prince are doing very well,' remarked Radinck.

She passed him his cup and saucer. 'Yes, aren't they? I went to see them this morning—twice, in fact... Oh, and I asked Juffrouw Kropp to see that your suit went to the cleaners.'

'I imagined you might; I emptied the pockets.' He stared at her so hard that she began to pinken, and to cover her guilty feelings about looking for that hanky, bent to lift the lid of the dish holding the scones.

'Will you have a scone?' she asked. 'Marta's such a wonderful cook...'

'And your dressing gown? That was ruined, I imagine.'

'Well, yes, but I think it'll clean—it may need several…'

'I don't think I should bother, Caroline.' He bent down and took the box from the floor beside his chair. 'I hope this will do instead.'

Caroline gave him a surprised look, undid the beribboned box slowly and gently lifted aside the layers of tissue paper, to lift out a pale pink quilted satin robe, its high neck and long sleeves edged with chiffon frills; the kind of extravagant garment she had so often stared at through shop windows and never hoped to possess.

'It's absolutely gorgeous!' she exclaimed. 'I shall love wearing it. Thank you very much, Radinck, it was most kind of you.' She smiled at him and just for once he smiled back at her.

They had a pleasant tea after that, not talking about anything much until Caro reminded him that they were to go to the burgermeester's reception the following evening.

'You have a dress?' Radinck enquired idly, 'or do you want to go to den Haag shopping—Noakes can easily drive you there.'

'Oh, I have a dress, thank you. It's—it's rather grand.'

'Too grand for my wife?' He spoke mockingly, but she didn't notice for once.

'Oh, oh, no, but it's rather—there's not a great deal of top to it.' She eyed him anxiously.

The corners of Radinck's stern mouth twitched. 'It was my impression that—er—not a great deal of top for the evening was all the fashion this season.'

'Well, it is. The sales lady said it was quite suitable, but I—I haven't been to an evening party for some time and I'm not sure…'

'The sales lady looked very knowledgeable,' said Radinck kindly, and forbore from adding that she would know better than to sell the Baroness Thoe van Erckelens anything unsuitable. 'Supposing you put it on and I'll take a look at it before we leave tomorrow—just to reassure you.'

'Oh, would you? I wouldn't like people to stare.' Caroline added reluctantly: 'I don't think I'm much good at parties.'

'Neither am I, Caroline, but you don't need to worry. Everyone is eager to meet a bride, you know.' His voice held a faint sneer and she winced and was only partly comforted by his: 'I'm sure the dress will be most suitable.'

Caro repeated this comforting observation to herself while she examined herself in the long mirror in her bedroom, dressed ready for the reception. There was no doubt about it, it was a beautiful dress; a pale smoky grey chiffon over satin with a finely pleated frill round its hem and the bodice which was causing her so much doubt, finely pleated too.

She turned away from her reflection, caught up the mink and went quickly down the staircase before she lost her nerve.

The drawing-room door was half open and Noakes, appearing from nowhere opened it wide for her to go through. Radinck was standing with his back to the hearth with Rex and Waterloo sitting at his feet enjoying the warmth. Caro nipped across the stretch of carpet and came to a breathless halt. 'Well?' she asked.

Radinck studied her leisurely. 'A charming dress,' he pronounced finally, 'exactly right for the occasion.'

She waited for him to say more, even a half-hearted compliment about herself would have been better than nothing at all, but he remained silent. And she had taken such pains with her face and hair and hands...

She said in a quiet little voice: 'I'm ready, Radinck,' and picked up her coat which Noakes had draped over a chair.

He didn't answer her but moved away from the fire to fetch something lying on one of the sofa tables. She thought how magnificent he looked in his tails and white tie, but if she told him so, he might think that she was wishing for a compliment in her turn.

He crossed the room to her, opened the case in his hand and took out its contents. 'This was my mother's,' he told her. 'I think it will go very well with this dress. Turn round while I fasten it for you.'

The touch of his fingers made her tremble although she stood obediently still, and then went to look in the great gilded mirror on one wall. The necklace was exquisite; sapphires linked by an intricate chain of diamonds, a dainty, costly trifle which went very well with her dress. She touched it lightly with a pretty hand, acknowledging its beauty and magnificence, while at the same time aware that if it had been a bead necklace from Woolworths given with all his love she would have worn it for ever and loved every bead.

She turned away from the mirror and got into the coat he was holding, picked up the grey satin purse which exactly matched her slippers and went with him to the car. On the way to Leeuwarden she asked: 'Is there anything special I should know about this evening?'

'I think not. I shall remain with you and see that you meet my friends, and once you have found your feet, I daresay you will like to talk to as many people as possible. It will be like any other party you have been to, Caroline.'

It was on the tip of her tongue to tell him that she had been to very few parties and certainly never to a grand reception, but pride curbed her tongue. She got out of the car presently, her determined little chin well up, and went up the steps to the burgermeester's front door, her skirts held daintily and with Radinck's hand under her elbow. She had a moment of panic in the enormous entrance hall as she was led away by a severe maid to remove her coat, and cast a longing look at the door—it was very close; she had only to turn and run...

'I shall be here waiting for you, Caroline,' said her husband quietly.

The reception rooms were on the first floor. Caroline went up the wide staircase, Radinck beside her, her heart beating fit to choke her. There were people all around them, murmuring and smiling, but Radinck didn't stop until they reached the big double doors opening on to the vast apartment where the burgermeester and his wife were receiving their guests. She had imagined that their host would be a large impressive man with a terrifying wife. He was nothing of the sort; of middle height and very stout, he had a fringe of grey hair and a round smiling face which beamed a welcome at her. She murmured politely in her carefully learned Dutch and was relieved when he addressed her in English.

'So, now I meet you, Baroness,' he chuckled, 'and how happy I am to do so. We will talk presently; I look forward to it.' He passed her on to his wife with a laughing remark to Radinck, who introduced her to a tall thin lady with a beaky nose and a sweet expression. Her English was fragmental and Caro, having repeated her few phrases, was relieved when Radinck took the conversation smoothly into his own hands before taking her arm and leading her into the room.

He seemed to know everyone there, and she shook hands and murmured, forgetting most of the names immediately until finally Radinck whisked her on to the floor to dance.

He danced well, but then so did she; not that she had had much chance to show her skill, but she had always loved dancing and it came naturally to her. She floated round in his arms, just for a little while a happy girl, although a peep at his face decided her not to talk. It was bland and faintly smiling, but the smile wasn't for her; she had the horrid feeling that he was doing his social duty without much pleasure. On the whole she was glad when the music stopped and Tiele and Becky joined them, and when the music started again it was Tiele who asked her to dance.

Unlike Radinck he chatted in an easy casual way, telling her how pretty she looked, how well she danced and wanting to know if she and Radinck would be at the hospital ball.

'Well, you know, I'm not sure about that—there

were so many invitations…' And when her partner looked surprised: 'Does Radinck always go?'

Tiele studied her earnest face carefully. 'Oh, yes, though it's always been a bit of a duty for him—not much fun for a man on his own, you know. But you're sure to be there this year. We must join forces for the evening.'

He was rewarded by her smile. 'I'd like that—it's all rather strange, you know, and my Dutch isn't up to much.'

'Never mind that,' he told her kindly. 'You dance like a dream and everyone's saying that you're just right for Radinck.'

She blushed brightly. 'Oh, thank you—I hope you're right; I don't mind what people say really, only I do want Radinck to be proud of me.'

Tiele's eyes were thoughtful, but he said easily: 'He's that all right!'

And after that Caroline went from partner to partner. There seemed to be no end to them, and although she caught glimpses of Radinck from time to time he made no attempt to approach her. It wasn't until they all went down to supper that he appeared suddenly beside her, took her arm and found her a seat at a table for four, before going in search of food at the buffet. Becky and Tiele, following them in, hesitated about joining them until Becky said softly: 'Look, darling, he's only danced with her once this evening. If it had been you I'd have boxed your ears! Look at her sitting there—she's lonely.'

'I'd rather look at you, my darling, and I don't think Radinck would like his ears boxed.'

'Well, of course he wouldn't, and Caro's clever enough to know that.' Becky added darkly: 'He's been leading a bachelor life too long—she's such a dear, too.'

'Which allows us to hope that he will become a happily married man, my love.'

Caro had seen them. Becky gave her husband's arm a wifely nip and obedient to this signal, they went to join her. Tiele said easily: 'Do you mind if we join you?' He settled his wife in a chair beside Caro. 'I suppose Radinck is battling his way towards the sandwiches—I'll join him.' He touched his wife lightly on her arm. 'Anything you fancy, darling?'

Becky thought briefly. 'Well, I like vol-au-vents, but only if they've got salmon in them, and those dear little cream puffs. What are you having, Caro?'

'I don't know.' Caro smiled brightly, wishing with all her heart that Radinck would call her darling in that kind of a voice and ask her what she would like, as though he really minded. Tiele, she felt sure, would bring back salmon vol-au-vents and cream puffs even if he had to go out and bake them himself.

But it seemed that these delicacies were readily

obtainable, for he was back in no time at all with a tray of food and Radinck with him. Caro accepted the chicken patties he had brought for her, had her glass filled with champagne and declared herself delighted with everything. And Radinck seemed to be enjoying himself, laughing and talking with Tiele and teasing Becky and treating herself with charming politeness. Only she wondered how much of it was social good manners, hiding his impatience of the whole evening. It wasn't until Becky remarked: 'We shall all see each other at the hospital ball, shan't we? Can't we go together?' that Caro saw the bland look on his face again and heard the sudden coolness in his voice.

'I'm not certain if we shall be going—I've that seminar in Vienna.'

'Isn't that on the following day?' asked Tiele.

'Yes, but I've one or two committees—I thought I'd go a day earlier and settle them first.' He glanced at Caro. 'I don't think Caroline will mind—we have so many parties during the next few weeks.'

Becky opened her mouth, caught her husband's quelling eye and closed it again, and Caro, anxious to do the right thing, observed with a cheerfulness she didn't feel that of course Radinck was quite right and she wouldn't mind missing the ball in the least.

'You could come with us,' suggested Becky, but was answered by Radinck's politely chilling:

'Might that not seem a little strange? We have been married for such a short time.'

'Oh, you mean that people might think you'd quarrelled or separated or something,' observed Becky forthrightly. 'Caro, let's go and tidy up for the second half,' and on their way: 'Caro, why don't you go to Vienna with Radinck?'

Caro tried to be nonchalant and failed utterly. 'Oh, he wouldn't want me around.' She went on quickly in case her companion got the wrong idea, 'He works so hard.' Which didn't quite seem adequate but was all she could think of.

Back on the dance floor, she almost gasped with relief when Radinck swept her into a waltz. She had been in a panic that he would introduce her to some dry-as-dust dignitary and leave her with him, or worse still, just leave her. They danced in silence for a few minutes before he asked her if she was enjoying herself.

'Yes, thank you,' said Caro. 'You have a great many friends, haven't you, and they are all very kind.'

'They have no reason to be otherwise.' He spoke so austerely that her champagne-induced pleasure dwindled away to nothing at all. She danced as she always did, gracefully and without fault, but her heart wasn't in it. Radinck was doing his duty again and not enjoying it, although she had to admit that nothing of his feelings showed on his face. The dance finished and he relinquished her to another partner and she didn't see him again until the last dance, when he swept her on to the floor again—but only, she thought sadly, because it was customary for the last dance to be enjoyed by married couples and sweethearts together.

They left quickly, giving Caro barely time to say goodbye to Becky. 'I'll telephone,' cried Becky, 'and anyway we'll see each other at the Hakelsmas' drinks party, won't we?'

Radinck maintained a steady flow of casual talk as they drove home. Caro listened when it seemed necessary and, once in the house, bade him a quiet goodnight and started up the staircase. She was halted halfway up by his query as to whether she wouldn't like a cup of coffee with him, but she paused only long enough to shake her head, glad that he was too far away to see the tears in her eyes. The evening, despite the dress, had been a failure. He had evinced no pleasure in her company and she had no doubt at all that the moment she was out of sight he would turn away with a sigh of thankfulness and go to his study, to immerse himself in his books and papers. She undressed very quickly and took off the necklace; tomorrow she would return it to him.

Ilke, not having been told otherwise, woke her early so that she might go riding, but she drank her tea slowly and then lay, listening for the sound of Rufus's hooves on the cobblestones. Presently, after they had died away, she got up, bathed and dressed in her new suit, did her face and hair and went down to her breakfast. Radinck was back by then, already halfway through his own meal, and she said at once as she went in: 'Good morning—no, don't get up, I'm sure you have no time.'

She slipped into her chair and sipped the coffee Noakes had poured for her and took a slice of toast.

'You were too tired to ride,' stated Radinck.

'Me, tired? Not in the least.' She gave him a sunny smile and buttered her toast, and after a moment or two he picked up his letters again, tossing several over to her as he did so.

'Will you answer these? Drinks mostly, I think.'

'You want me to refuse them?'

He looked impatient. 'Certainly not. Why should you think that?'

Caroline didn't answer. After all, she had told him once; she wasn't going to keep on. Instead she got on with her breakfast and when Noakes went out of the room, she got up and put the necklace carefully beside her husband's plate.

'Thank you for letting me wear it,' she said.

He put down the letter he had been reading to stare at her down his handsome nose. 'My dear Caroline, I gave it to you.'

She opened her hazel eyes wide. 'Oh, did you? I thought you'd lent it to me just for the evening. How kind—but I can't accept it, you know.'

'Why not?' Radinck's brows were drawn together in an ominous frown.

She did her best to explain. 'Well, it's not like a present, is it? I mean, one gives a present because one wants to, but you gave me the necklace to wear because your wife would be expected to have the family jewels.'

Radinck crumpled up the letter in his hand and hurled it at the wastepaper basket.

'What an abominable girl you are, Caroline! As I said some time ago, you have this gift of putting me in the wrong.'

'I'm sorry if you're annoyed, but I can't possibly accept it, though I'll wear any jewellery you like when we go out together.'

He said silkily: 'Don't count on going out too often, Caroline, I'm a busy man.'

'Well, I wasn't going to.' She gave him a thoughtful look, and added kindly: 'You're very cross—I daresay you're tired. We should have left earlier last night.'

The silkiness was still there, tinged with ice now. 'When I wish you to organise my life, Caroline, I will say so. I am not yet so elderly that I cannot decide things for myself.'

'Oh, you're not elderly at all,' said Caro sooth-ingly. 'You're not even middle-aged. How silly of you to think that; you must know that you're…' She stopped abruptly and he urged her blandly:

'Do go on.'

'No, I won't, you'll only bite my head off if I do.' She took a roll and spread it with butter and cheese. 'What time do you want to go to Mevrouw Hakelsma's party? Only so that I'll be ready on time,' she added hastily.

'It is for half past seven, isn't it? I should be home by six o'clock. Will you see that dinner is later?'

'Would half past eight suit you? I'll tell Juffrouw Kropp.'

He nodded. 'I should like to leave the Hakelsmas' place within an hour; I've a good deal of work wait-ing.'

Caro kept her face cheerful. 'Of course. Just nod and wink at me when you're ready to leave.'

Radinck got up from the table. 'I shall neither nod nor wink,' he told her cuttingly. 'You are my wife, not the dog.' He stalked to the door. 'I'll see you this evening.'

She said, 'Yes, Radinck,' so meekly that he shot her a suspicious look and paused to say:

'It will be short dresses this evening.'

She said 'Yes, Radinck,' again, still so meek that he exclaimed forcefully:

'I wish you would refrain from this continuous "Yes, Radinck", as though I were a tyrant!'

'Oh, but you're not,' Caro assured him warmly. 'That's the last thing you are; it's just that you've lived so long alone that you've forgotten how to talk. Never mind, you'll soon get into the habit again now that I'm here.' She gave him a limpid smile and he said something in a subdued roar, something nasty in his own language, she judged, as she watched him go.

She finished her breakfast, inspected more cup-boards under Juffrouw Kropp's guidance, discussed the evening's dinner with Marta and then arranged the flowers, a task she enjoyed even though it took a long time, and then went down to see how Queenie was getting on. Willem was there and they stood admiring the little donkey and her son, carry-ing on a conversation, which, while completely un-grammatical on Caro's part, Willem understood very well. She had sugar for the horses too, and Jemmy whinnied when he saw her, looking at her so re-proachfully that she changed after lunch and, with Jan keeping a watchful eye on her, rode round the fields. Which didn't leave her much time for any-thing else. She was ready, wearing one of her new dresses, pink silk jersey with a demure neck and long sleeves, well before six o'clock, and went to sit in the smaller of the sitting-rooms, industriously knitting. It was half past six when Noakes came to tell her that Radinck was on the telephone.

He sounded austere. 'I'm sorry, Caroline, but I shall be home later than I expected. Perhaps you could ring Mevrouw Hakelsma and say all the right things. I don't expect we can get there much before eight o'clock.'

She said, 'Yes, Radinck,' before she could stop herself, but what else was there to say? 'OK, darling,' wouldn't have pleased him at all. She went along to the kitchen and prudently arranged for dinner to be delayed, then went back to her knitting.

Radinck got home at half past seven, looking tired, which somehow made him more approachable.

Caro wished him a pleasant good evening. 'Would you like a sandwich before you go upstairs?' she asked.

He had gone to the sofa table where the tray of drinks was. 'Thank you, I should—I missed lunch. What will you drink?'

'Sherry, thank you.' She pressed the old-fashioned brass bell beside the hearth and when Noakes came asked for a plate of sandwiches.

Radinck was famished. He devoured the lot with his whisky, looking like a tired, very handsome wolf who hadn't had a square meal for days. Caro watching him, bursting with love, sighed soundlessly; he needed someone to look after him so badly.

He went away presently, to rejoin her in a little while looking immaculate in one of his beautifully cut dark suits. She got up at once, laid her knitting on the work table and went with him into the hall where Noakes was waiting with their coats. Radinck helped her into hers and shrugged on his own coat, and Caro, with a quick whisper to Noakes to be sure and have dinner ready to put on the table the moment they got back, followed Radinck out to the car.

The Hakelsmas lived on the outskirts of Leeuwarden, in a large red-brick villa full of heavy, comfortable furniture. Caro had already met them at the burgermeester's reception and liked them both—in their forties, jolly, plump and kind. They had a large family, and three of them were there helping to entertain the guests, of whom there seemed to be a great many.

Caro murmured her set piece to her host and hostess, accepted a glass of sherry and something called a *bitterbal* which she didn't like at all, and was swept away to go from one group to the other, careful never to lose sight of Radinck. He seemed very popular, laughing and talking as though he liked nothing better than standing about drinking sherry and making small talk, and some of the girls there were very pretty and he appeared to be on very good terms with them. Caro, swept by a wave of jealousy, tried

not to look at him too much. She had never thought
of him as being likely to fall in love with anyone else,
but there was no earthly reason why he shouldn't.
One couldn't help these things. Of course she had
every intention of trying to make him fall in love with
her, but she began to wonder if the competition was
too keen. Her not very pleasant thoughts were interrupted by Becky's voice.

'Hullo—you're looking wistful. Why?' She
beamed at Caro. 'You're late. Did Radinck get held
up?'

'Yes. There are a lot of people here, aren't there?
I expect I met most of them at the burgermeester's.'

'Don't worry, it took me months to remember
everyone's name, but they're all very sweet about it,
and we'll all be seeing each other quite a lot during
the next few weeks. Radinck gave an enormous party
last year—are you having one this year too?'

'I think so.'

'Well, I expect now he's got you, he'll go out
more. He's always been a bit of a recluse—well,
ever since…'

'His first wife died? That's understandable, isn't
it?' Caro smiled at Becky and let her see that she
knew all about the first wife and it didn't matter at
all.

On their way home presently, she said carefully:
'Radinck, I don't a bit mind not going to all these

parties if you don't want to. After all, everyone knows you're a very busy man—mind you,' she observed thoughtfully, 'I daresay you don't need to do as much work as you do, if you see what I mean. Becky said you didn't go out much before—before we got married, and I did promise you that I'd not interfere with your life…'

She couldn't see his face, but she could tell from his voice that he was frowning. 'I thought that I had made myself clear; we will attend as many of these parties as possible, give an evening party ourselves, and then I shall be able to return to what you call my life. For most of the year there is very little social life on a big scale, only just before Christmas and at the New Year. Once that is over…' He slowed the car a little and Caro, thankful for the chance to talk to him even if only for a brief while, said unhappily: 'You hate it, don't you? I'm glad it's only for a few weeks. What a pity I can't get 'flu or something, then we couldn't go…'

'That is a singularly foolish remark, Caroline. Of course you won't get anything of the sort.'

But just for once he, who was so often right, was wrong. Caro woke up in the morning feeling faintly peculiar. She hadn't got a headache, but her head felt heavy, and moreover, when she got out of bed her feet didn't seem to touch the ground. She had no appetite for her breakfast either, but as Radinck was reading his letters and scanning the morning's papers, she didn't think that mattered. He was never chatty over the meal; she took some toast and crumbled it at intervals just in case he should look up, and drank several cups of coffee which revived her sufficiently to bid him goodbye in a perfectly normal way. They weren't going anywhere that evening and she would be able to go to bed early, as he so often went straight to his study after dinner. She went through her morning routine, visited Queenie and Prince, took Waterloo for a brief walk in the gardens and retired to the library to struggle with her Dutch. But she didn't seem able to concentrate, not even with the help of several more cups of coffee. She toyed with her lunch, which upset Noakes very much, and then went back to the sitting-room, got out her knitting and curled up in Radinck's chair with Waterloo on her lap. He was warm and comforting and after a very short time she gave up trying to knit and closed her eyes and dozed off into a troubled sleep, to be wakened by a worried Noakes with the tea tray.

'Yer not yerself, ma'am,' he declared. 'Yer ought to go ter bed.'

She eyed him hazily. 'Yes, I think I will when I've had tea, Noakes. It's just a cold.'

She drank the teapot dry and went off to sleep again, her cheeks flushed and her head heavy. She didn't wake when Radinck, met at the door by an anxious Noakes, came into the room.

Caro looked small and lonely and lost in his great chair and he muttered something as he bent over her, a cool hand on her hot forehead. She woke up then, staring into the blue eyes so close to hers. 'I feel very grotty,' she mumbled. 'I meant to go to bed... I'll go now.'

She began to scramble out of the chair and he picked her up with Waterloo still in her arms. 'You should have gone hours ago,' he said almost angrily. 'You weren't well at breakfast—why didn't you say so then?'

He was mounting the staircase and she muttered: 'I can walk,' and then: 'I thought I'd feel better. Besides, I didn't think you noticed.'

Noakes had gone ahead to open the door and Radinck laid her on the bed, asked Noakes to fetch Juffrouw Kropp and then pulled the coverlet over Caro, who was beginning to shiver. 'So sorry,' she told him, 'such a nuisance for you. I'll be quite all right now.'

He didn't answer but waited until Juffrouw Kropp came into the room, spoke to her quietly and went away, while that lady undressed Caro as though she had been a baby, tucked her up in her bed and went to fetch Radinck, walking up and down the gallery outside. Caro, feeling so wretched by now that she didn't care about anything at all, put out her tongue, muttered and mumbled ninety-nine and then swallowed the pills she was given. She was asleep in five minutes.

She woke a couple of hours later, feeling very peculiar in the head, and found Radinck bending over her again. He looked large and solid and very dependable, and she sighed with relief because he was there.

'Now you won't have to go to the party tomorrow,' she told him, still half asleep, 'and there's a dinner party…when? Quite soon; we needn't go to that either.' She closed her eyes and then opened them wide again. 'I'm so glad, you can have peace and quiet again.'

She dropped off again, so that she didn't hear the words wrung so reluctantly from Radinck's lips. Which was a pity.

She felt a little better in the morning, but her recollection of the night was hazy; she had wakened several times and there had been a lamp by the bed, but the rest of the room had been in shadow. And once or twice someone had given her a drink, but she had been too tired to open her eyes and see who it was. Radinck came to see her at breakfast time, pronounced himself satisfied as to her progress and went away again, leaving her with Waterloo for company. Presently Juffrouw Kropp came and washed her face and hands, brushed her hair and then brought her a tray of tea—nice strong tea with a lot of milk, and paper-thin bread and butter.

Caro dozed through the day. Lovingly tended by Juffrouw Kropp, Marta and the maids, it seemed to her that each time she opened her eyes there was someone in the room looking anxiously at her. Towards teatime Noakes came in with a vase of autumn flowers and a message from Becky and Tiele, and that was followed by a succession of notes and several more flower arrangements.

'But I've only got 'flu,' said Caro. 'I mean, there's really no need…'

'Very well liked, yer are, ma'am,' said Noakes with deep satisfaction. 'The phone's bin going on and off all afternoon with messages.'

'But how did they all know?'

'The Professor will 'ave cancelled your engagements, ma'am.'

Caro nodded. She wasn't enjoying having 'flu, but at least it was making Radinck happy. She drank her tea and after a struggle to keep awake, slept again.

She woke to find Radinck at the foot of the bed, looking at her, and she assured him before he could ask her that she was feeling a great deal better. She sat up against the pillows, happily unaware of her wan face and tousled hair. 'And look at all these flowers,' she begged him, 'and I'm not even ill. I feel a fraud!'

He said seriously: 'You have no need to—you have a quite violent virus infection of the respiratory system.'

It was silly to get upset, but somehow he had made her feel like a patient in a hospital bed; someone to be cured of an ailment with a completely impersonal care. Her eyes filled with tears until they dripped down her cheeks and although she put up an impatient hand to rub them away, there seemed no end to them. Radinck bent over her, a handkerchief in his hand, but she pushed it away. 'I'm perfectly all right,' she told him crossly. 'It's just that I don't feel quite the thing.' She added peevishly: 'I think I'd like to go to sleep.'

She closed her eyes so that he would see that she really meant that, and although the tears were still pouring from under her lids, she kept them shut. And after a minute or so she really did feel sleepy in a dreamy kind of way, so that the kiss on her cheek seemed part of the dream too. She woke much later and remembered it—it had been very pleasant; dreams could be delightful. She dismissed the idea that Radinck had kissed her as ridiculous and wept a little before she slept again.

CHAPTER EIGHT

TWO DAYS LATER Caro was on her feet again. She had been coddled and mothered by Juffrouw and Marta, ably backed by the maids and old Jan who sent in flowers each day from his cherished hot-houses, the whole team masterminded by Noakes. No one could have been kinder. Even Radinck, visiting her twice a day, had been meticulous in his attentions. Although that hadn't stopped him telling her that he would be going to Vienna that evening. 'You wouldn't wish to go to the hospital ball,' he pointed out with unescapable logic, 'and much though I regret having to leave you while you are feeling under the weather, my presence is hardly necessary to your recovery. My entire—I beg your pardon—our entire staff are falling over themselves to lavish attention upon you.' He gave her a mocking little smile. 'I leave you in the best of hands.'

Caro had agreed with him in a quiet little voice.

Normally she wouldn't have allowed herself to feel crushed by his high-handedness, but she wasn't quite herself. Her chances of making him fall in love with her seemed so low they hardly bore contemplation. She wished him goodbye and hoped he would have a good trip and that the seminar would be interesting, and then, unable to think of anything else to say, sat up in bed just looking at him.

'Goodbye, Caroline,' said Radinck in a quite different voice, and bent and kissed her cheek. She didn't move for quite a while after he had gone, but presently when Waterloo jumped on to the bed and gave her an enquiring butt with his head, she scratched the top of it in an absent manner. 'I didn't dream it, then,' she told him. 'He kissed me then as well. Now, I wonder…'

It was probably a false hope, but at least she could work on it. She got bathed and dressed and went downstairs, to be fussed over by everyone in the house, and all of them remarked how much better she looked.

She felt better. Somewhere or other there was a chink in her husband's armour of cool aloofness; she would have to work on it. Much cheered by the thought, she spent her day catching up on her Dutch, knitting like a fury and entertaining Rex, who with his master gone, was feeling miserable.

'Well, I feel the same,' Caro told him, 'and at least

he's glad to see you when he comes home.' She insisted on going to the servants' sitting-room to rehearse the carols after dinner too, although Noakes shook his head and said she ought to be in bed.

'Well, yes, I'm sure you're right,' Caro agreed, 'but Christmas is getting close and we do want to put on a perfect performance. I think that tomorrow evening we'd better get together in the drawing-room so that you'll all know where to stand and so on. The moment the Professor comes home on Christmas Eve, you can all file in and take up your places and the minute he comes into the room you can start. It should be a lovely surprise.'

She went to bed quite happy presently with Waterloo to keep her company and Juffrouw Kropp coming in with hot milk to sip so that she would sleep and strict instructions to ring if she wanted anything during the night.

They were all such dears, thought Caro, curled up cosily in the centre of the vast bed. Life could have been wonderful if only Radinck had loved her even a little. But that was no way to think, she scolded herself. 'Faint heart never won Radinck,' she told Waterloo, on the edge of sleep.

The weather was becoming very wintry. She woke in the morning to grey, woolly clouds, heavy with snow and the sound of the wind racing through the bare trees near the house. But the great house was

warm and very comfortable and she spent her morning doing the flowers once again, with Jan bringing
her armsful of them from his hothouses. There was
Marta to talk to about the meals too; something special for dinner on the following day when Radinck
would return. The day passed quickly. Caroline ate
her dinner with appetite with Noakes brooding over
her in a fatherly way, then repaired to the drawing-
room.

They were all a little shy at first. The room was
grand and they felt stiff and awkward and out of
place until Caro said in her sparse, excruciating
Dutch: 'Sing as though you were in your own sitting-
room—remember it's to give the Professor pleasure
and it's only because this is the best place for him to
hear you.'

They loosened up after that. They were well embarked on *Silent Night* with all the harmonies just
right, when the Professor unlocked his own front
door. No one heard him. Even Rex, dozing by the
fire, was deafened by the choir. He stood for a moment in the centre of the hall and then walked very
quietly to the drawing-room door, not quite closed.
The room was in shadow with only a lamp by the
piano and the sconces on either side of the fireplace
alight. He pushed the door cautiously a few inches
so that he could look in and no one saw him. They
were grouped round Caro at the piano, her mousy

head lighted by the lamp beside her, one hand beating time while the other thumped out the tune. Radinck closed the door gently again and retreated to where he had cast down his coat and bag and let himself out of the house again. The car's engine made no noise above the sighing and whistling of the wind. He drove back the way he had come, all the way to the airport on the outskirts of Leeuwarden where he parked the car, telephoned his home that he had returned earlier than he had expected, then got back into the car and, for the second time, drove himself home.

Caro had received the news of Radinck's unexpected return with outward calm. 'We'll find time to rehearse again tomorrow,' she told them all. 'Now I think if Marta would warm up some of that delicious soup just in case the Professor's cold and hungry…'

She closed the piano and went to sit in the sitting-room by the fire, her tapestry in her hands. She even had time to do a row or two before she heard Radinck open the door, speak to Noakes, on the watch for him, and cross the hall to open the sitting-room door.

'What a nice surprise!' she smiled as he came into the room. 'Would you like dinner or just soup and sandwiches?'

'Coffee will do, thank you, Caroline.' He sat down

opposite her. 'You are feeling better, I can see that, and being sensible, sitting quietly here.'

'Oh, I've been very sensible,' she assured him. 'Would you like coffee in your study?'

He looked annoyed. 'My dear girl, I have just this minute returned home and here you are, banishing me to my study!'

Caro went red. 'I'm sorry, I didn't mean it like that, only you so often do go there—I thought you might rather be alone.'

'Very considerate of you; I prefer to remain here. What have you been doing with yourself?'

'Oh, almost nothing—the flowers and catching up with my Dutch, and showing Marta how to make mince pies...'

'I surprised you playing the piano before we married,' he said. 'Do you remember? Don't you play any more?'

Caro's red face went pale. 'Yes—well, sometimes I do.'

He sat back in his chair, relaxed and at ease, and watched while Noakes placed the coffee tray at Caro's elbow. 'Have you any plans for Christmas?' he asked idly.

She stammered a little. 'I understand from Noakes that you don't—that is, you prefer a quiet time.'

'I am afraid that over the years I have got into the habit of doing very little about entertaining—I did

mention the party which I give, did I not? Is there
anything special you would enjoy? A little music
perhaps?'

'Music?' Caro's needle was working overtime,
regardless of wrong stitches. She took a deep breath.
'Oh, you mean going to concerts and that sort of
thing; Becky was telling me…but you really don't
have to bother. We did agree when we married that
your life wasn't to be changed at all, but you've already had to go to these parties with me and you
must have disliked them very much. I'm very happy,
you know, I don't mind if I don't go out socially.'

'I thought girls liked dressing up and going out to
parties.'

'Well, yes, of course, but you see I don't enjoy
them if you don't.' She hadn't meant to say that. She
stitched a whole row, her head bowed over her work,
and wished fruitlessly that the floor would open and
swallow her up.

'And what precisely do you mean by that?' asked
Radinck blandly.

'Nothing, nothing at all.' And then, knowing that she
wouldn't get away with that, she added: 'What I meant
was that I feel guilty because you have to give up your
evenings doing something you don't enjoy when you
might be in your study reading…and writing.'

'Put like that I seem to be a very selfish man. I
must endeavour to make amends.'

Caro gave him a surprised glance. He wasn't being sarcastic and his voice held a warm note she hadn't heard before.

'You're not selfish,' she told him in a motherly voice. 'No one would expect you to change your whole way of life, certainly I wouldn't. You've devoted yourself to your work and the staff adore you—so do the animals.'

'And what about you, Caroline?'

She took her time answering. 'You must know that I have a great regard for you, Radinck.' She looked across at him, her loving heart in her eyes and unaware of it. 'You have no need to reproach yourself; you made it very clear before we married that you didn't want to change your life, and I agreed to that. I'm very content.'

His eyes were searching. 'Are you? Perhaps I have done wrong in marrying you, Caroline—you might have found some younger man...'

'I wish you wouldn't keep harping on your great age!' declared Caro hotly. Suddenly she could stand no more of it. She threw down her embroidery carelessly, so that the wools flew in all directions, and hurried out of the room and up to her bedroom, where she burst into tears, making Waterloo's fur very damp while she hugged him. 'What am I going to do?' she asked him. 'One minute I think he likes me a little and then he says he regrets marrying me…' Which wasn't quite true, although that was how it seemed to her.

She went to bed because there was nothing else to do, but she didn't go to sleep; she lay listening to the now familiar sounds in the old house—the very faint clatter from the kitchens, Rex's occasional bark, the tread of Noakes' rather heavy feet crossing the hall, the subdued clang as he closed the gate leading to the garden from the side door, even faint horsey noises from the stables. It was a clear, cold night, and sounds carried. Presently she heard Noakes and Marta and the rest of them going up the back stairs at the end of the gallery on their way to bed, and after that the house was quiet save for the various clocks striking the hour, each in its own good time.

It was almost one o'clock and she was still awake when she heard cars travelling fast along the road at the end of the drive, and the next moment there was a kind of slow-motion crashing and banging and the sound of glass splintering and then distant faint cries. She was out of bed and pulling back the curtains within seconds and saw lights shine out as the front door was opened and Radinck went running down the drive, his bag in his hand. Caroline didn't stop to take off her nightie but pulled on a pair of slacks, bundled a sweater on top of them, and rushed downstairs in her bare feet. Her wellingtons were in one of the hall cupboards; she got into them just as

Noakes came down the stairs with a dressing gown over his pyjamas.

'You'll need a coat, Noakes,' said Caro, 'and thick shoes, it's cold outside, then will you come to the gate and see if the Professor wants you to telephone.' She didn't wait for him to reply but opened the door and started down the drive. Something was on fire now, she could smell it and see the flickering of flames somewhere on the road to the left of the gates. But there were no cries any more, although she thought she could hear voices.

There were two cars, hopelessly entangled, and one was blazing with thick black smoke pouring from it. Well away from it there were people on the grass verge of the road, some sitting and two lying, and she could see Radinck bending over them. She fetched up beside him, took the torch he was holding from him and shone it on the man lying on the ground. 'Noakes is coming as soon as he's got his coat on,' she said quietly.

'Good girl!' He was on his knees now, opening the man's jacket. 'Shine the light here, will you? There are scissors in my bag, can you reach them?'

Noakes arrived then, out of breath but calmly dignified. He listened to what Radinck had to say and with a brisk: 'OK, Professor,' turned and went back again. 'And bring some blankets and towels with you!' shouted Radinck after him.

The man was unconscious with head injuries and a fractured pelvis. They made him as comfortable as they could and moved on to the other silent figure close by. Head injuries again, and Radinck grunted as he bent to examine him, but beyond telling Caro to wrap one of the towels Noakes had brought back round the man's head and covering him with a blanket he did nothing. There were three people sitting on the frosty grass—an elderly man, a woman of the same age and a girl. Radinck looked at the older woman first, questioning her quietly as he did so. 'Shock,' he said to Caro, 'and a fractured clavicle— fix it with a towel, will you?' He moved on to the man, examined him briefly, said, 'Shock and no injuries apparent,' and then bent over the girl.

The loveliest girl Caro had ever set eyes on; small and fair with great blue eyes, and even with her hair all over the place and a dirty face she was breathtaking. 'Were you driving?' asked Radinck.

It was a pity that Caro's Dutch didn't stretch to understanding what the girl answered, nor, for that matter, what Radinck said after that. She held the torch, handed him what he wanted from his bag and wished with all her heart that she was even half as lovely as the girl sitting between them. She had looked at Radinck's face just once and although it wore the bland mask of his profession, she knew that he found the girl just as beautiful as she did; he would have been a strange man if he hadn't. The girl said something to him in a low voice and he answered her gently, putting an arm round her slim shoulders, smiling at her and then, to Caro's eyes at least, getting to his feet with reluctance.

'Stay with them, will you, Caroline?—this poor girl's had a bad shock, the others aren't too bad. I'll take a look at the other two, though there's nothing much to be done until we get them to hospital.' He stood listening for a moment. 'There are the ambulances now.'

He went away then and presently as the two ambulances slowed to a halt, Caro saw him directing the loading of the two unconscious men. The first ambulance went away and he came over to where she was waiting with the other three casualties. 'Go back to the house,' he told her. 'There's nothing more you can do. Get a warm drink and go to bed. I'll follow these people in to the hospital, there may be something I can do.' She hesitated, suddenly feeling unwanted and longing for a reassuring word. He had spoken briskly, as he might have spoken to a casual stranger who had stopped to give a hand, only she felt sure that he would have added his thanks.

'Do as I say, Caroline!' and this time he sounded urgent and coldly angry. She turned without a word and went down the drive, her feet and hands numb with cold, and climbed the steps slowly to where Juffrouw Kropp was waiting, wrapped in a dressing gown, and any neglect she had suffered at her husband's hands was instantly made up for by the care and attention she now received. Hardly knowing what was happening, she was bustled upstairs and into bed where Juffrouw Kropp tucked her in as though she had been a small girl and Marta waited with a tray of hot drinks. Both ladies stood one each side of the bed, while she sipped hot milk and brandy, reassured themselves that she had come to no harm and then told her firmly to go to sleep and not to get up in the morning until one or both of them had been to see her.

'But I'm not ill,' protested Caro weakly.

'You have had the grippe,' Juffrouw Kropp pointed out. 'The Professor will never forgive us if you are ill again.'

Caro searched her muddled head for the right words. 'He's gone to the hospital—he'll be late and cold…'

'Do not worry, Baroness, he will be cared for when he returns. Now you will sleep.'

'I ought to be there.' Caro spoke in English, not caring whether she was understood or not.

'No, no, he would not like that.'

She gave up and closed her eyes, not knowing that while Marta crept out with the tray, Juffrouw Kropp perched herself on the edge of a chair and waited until she was quite sure that Caro slept.

She wakened to find that lady standing at the foot of the bed, looking at her anxiously, but the anxious look went as Caroline sat up in bed and said good morning and then gave a small shriek when she saw the time.

'Ten o'clock?' she exclaimed, horrified. 'Why didn't someone call me? Is the Professor back?'

Juffrouw Kropp shook her head. 'He telephoned, Baroness. He will be back perhaps this afternoon, perhaps later.'

Caro plastered a cheerful smile on her face. 'Oh, yes, of course, he'll be busy. I'll get up.'

'Marta brings your breakfast at once—there is no need for you to get up, *mevrouw*, it will snow before long and it is very cold outside.'

Under Juffrouw Kropp's eagle eye Caro put her foot back in bed. 'Well, it would be nice,' she conceded. The housekeeper smiled in a satisfied way and shook up the pillows.

'There has been a telephone call for you— Baroness Raukema van den Eck—she heard about the accident. I asked her to telephone later, Baroness. She hopes that you are all right.'

It was nice to have a friend, reflected Caro, sitting up in bed eating a splendid breakfast, someone who wanted to know how you were and really minded. Not like Radinck. She choked on a piece of toast and pushed the tray away and got up.

It wasn't until the afternoon that Radinck telephoned, and by then any number of people had rung up. Becky, of course, wanting to know exactly what had happened, asking if Caroline were quite better, did she need anything, would she like to go over and see them soon. 'Tiele saw Radinck for a few minutes this morning,' went on Becky. 'He was getting ready to drive one of the crash people home—the girl who was driving. You'll know that, of course. I must say it's pretty good of him to go all the way to Dordrecht with her—let's hope the snow doesn't get any worse.'

Caro had made some suitable reply and put down the phone very thoughtfully. Of course, there might be some very good reason why Radinck should take the girl back home—something urgent—but there were trains, and cars to hire and buses, and most people had friends or family who rallied round at such a time. She did her best to forget about it, answered suitably when a number of other people she had met at the burgermeester's reception telephoned, took Rex for a quick walk in the garden, despite Juffrouw Kropp's protests that she would catch her death of cold, and settled down by the fire to con her Dutch lessons.

The weather worsened as the day wore on; it was snowing hard by the time Radinck telephoned. He sounded cool and rather casual and Caroline did her best to be the same. 'I'm in Dordrecht,' he told her. 'I took Juffrouw van Doorn back to her home; she had no way of reaching it otherwise and her parents must stay in hospital for a few days. I shall do my best to get back this evening, but the weather isn't too good.'

'It's snowing hard here,' said Caro, anxious not to sound anxious. 'If you'd rather not drive back—I expect you can find a hotel or something.'

'Juffrouw van Doorn has offered me a bed for the night—probably I shall accept it. You're all right?'

'Perfectly, thank you.' And even if I weren't, she added silently, I wouldn't tell you. 'Do you want me to tell anyone? Have you any appointments for the morning?'

His low laugh came very clearly over the wire. 'Really, Caroline, you are becoming the perfect wife! No, there's no one you need telephone. I can do it all from here.'

'Very well—we'll expect you when we see you.'

'Caroline—about last night—'

She interrupted him ruthlessly. 'I'm sorry, I must go. Goodbye, Radinck.'

The rest of the day was a dead loss.

They were to go to a party the following evening. Becky had telephoned to know if they were going and Caro had improvised hurriedly and said that they expected to be there but Radinck would let her know the moment he could leave Dordrecht. 'The weather's awful there,' she invented, 'and I told him not to come home until the roads were clear.'

And Becky had said how wise she was and she hoped they'd see each other the next day.

There was no word from Radinck the next day. Caro ordered the meals as though he were expected home, took Rex for a snowy walk, rehearsed her choir and then telephoned the people whose party they were to attend and made their excuses. She was on the rug before the fire in the sitting-room when Radinck walked in, with Waterloo purring beside her and Rex leaning heavily against her. He bounded to the door as Radinck came in and Caro looked round and then got slowly to her feet. 'You didn't telephone,' she observed, quite forgetting to say hullo.

'No, I'm sorry I couldn't get back sooner—the roads are bad.' He fended Rex off with a gentle hand and sat down. 'How quiet and peaceful you look, Caroline.'

Appearances can be deceptive, she thought. She wasn't either, inside her she boiled with rage and misery and jealousy and all the other things which were supposed to be so bad for one. 'I hope the trip wasn't too bad,' she remarked. 'Would you like some coffee?'

'Yes, thanks. Aren't we supposed to be going to the Laggemaats' this evening?'

'Yes, but I telephoned them about an hour ago and told them that as you weren't back we would probably not be able to go. I hope I did right.'

'Quite right. Did you not wonder where I was?'

She said evenly: 'When we married you particularly stressed the fact that that was something I was never to do.'

She poured the coffee Noakes had brought and handed Radinck a cup.

He said testily: 'You seem to have remembered every word I said and moreover, are determined to keep to it.'

Caroline didn't answer that but asked in her quiet little voice: 'How are the people who were hurt in the accident?'

'The first man is in intensive care, the second man died on the way to hospital—I think you may have guessed that; the two older people who were in the second car are to remain under observation for another day or so. Their daughter—Ilena—I drove home.'

Caro busied herself pouring a cup of coffee she didn't want. 'Oh, yes, Becky told me when she telephoned yesterday.' She was careful to keep all traces of reproach from her voice. 'I'm so glad she wasn't hurt; she was the loveliest girl I've ever seen.'

'Extraordinarily beautiful,' agreed Radinck blandly, 'and so young, too. She asked me to stay the night and I did.'

'Very sensible of you,' declared Caro calmly. 'Travelling back in all that snow would never have done.'

'What would you say if I told you that I've never allowed bad weather to interfere with my driving?'

She could say a great many things, thought Caro, and all of them very much to the point. She didn't utter any of them but said prudently: 'I think it was very wise of you to make an exception to your rule.'

She put down her coffee cup and picked up her work again, glad to be able to busy herself with something.

Radinck stretched out his legs and wedged his great shoulders deeply into his chair. 'Don't you want to know why I took Ilena home?'

'You must have had a good reason for doing so—I daresay she was badly shaken and not fit to travel on her own.'

'She was perfectly able to go on her own. I drove her because I wanted to prove something to myself.' He frowned. 'I seem to be in some confusion of mind—about you, Caroline.'

She looked up from her work, her eyes thoughtful as she studied his handsome and, at the moment, ill-tempered face. Her heart was thundering against her ribs. That he was about to say something important was evident, but what, exactly? She had promised herself that she would make him love her, but it seemed probable that she had failed and he was going to tell her so. She said steadily: 'If you want to talk about it I'm listening, Radinck.'

It was a pity that just at that moment the telephone on the table beside him should ring. He lifted the receiver and listened, frowning, and then embarked on what Caro took to be a list of instructions about a patient. The interruption gave her time to collect her thoughts, which were, however, instantly scattered by the entry of Noakes, announcing Tiele and Becky.

'We were on our way to the Laggemaats',' explained Becky, 'and Tiele thought it would be an idea to pop in and see how you were.'

She kissed Caro, offered a cheek to Radinck and perched herself on a chair close to Caro, spreading the skirts of her dress as she did so.

'That's pretty,' observed Caro. 'It's new, isn't it? I love the colour. I was going to wear a rather nice green...'

Tiele had bent to kiss her cheek and said laughingly: 'Oh, lord—clothes again! Radinck, take me to your study and show me that agenda for the seminar at Brussels. Are you going? We could go together—we need only be away for a couple of days.'

The two men went away and Becky, declining coffee, remarked: 'We weren't sure if Radinck would be back. The roads are very bad further south. He telephoned Tiele about some patient or other quite late last night—said he'd gone to a hotel in Dordrecht and planned to leave early this morning, but he got held up—you know all that, of course.' She ate one of the small biscuits on the coffee tray. 'He must have been glad to have handed that girl over to her aunt—a bit of a responsibility—supposing he'd got landed in a snowdrift!' She giggled engagingly.

Caro had listened to this artless information in surprise and a mounting excitement. If what Becky had told her was true, why had Radinck let her think that he'd stayed at the girl's house? Had he wanted to make her jealous? On the other hand, did he want her to believe that he had thought better of their dry-as-dust marriage and wanted to put an end to it? More likely the latter, she considered, although that was something she would have to find out. She wasn't sure how and she had a nasty feeling that whatever it was Radinck had been going to say wouldn't be said—at least not for the moment.

In this she was perfectly right. The van den Ecks went presently and Radinck went almost at once to his study with the observation that he had a good deal of paperwork to do. Which left Caro with nothing better to do than go to bed.

CHAPTER NINE

THE SNOW LAY thick on the ground when Caro looked out of her windows in the morning. It was barely light and she could see Radinck, huge in a sheepskin jacket, striding down to the stables with Rex at his heels. He would be going to see how Queenie fared before walking Rex in the fields beyond. It would have been lovely to be with him, she thought, walking in the early morning cold, talking about his work and planning a pleasant evening together. Which reminded her that there was another party that evening and presumably they would be going: a doctor from the hospital and his wife—she searched her memory and came up with their name—ter Brink, youngish if she remembered aright and rather nice. She would have to ring Becky and ask what she should wear. She bathed and dressed and went downstairs and found Radinck already at the table.

It was hardly the time or place to expect him to disclose what he had intended to say to her, but she sat down hopefully and began her breakfast. But beyond a polite good morning, the hope that she had slept well, and could he pass her the toast, he had nothing to say, but became immersed in his letters once again. Caroline was glad that she had a modest pile of post beside her plate for once. It seemed to keep her occupied and by reading each letter two or three times, she spun out her interest in them until Radinck put his own mail down and got to his feet.

'You feel well enough to go to the ter Brinks' this evening?' he asked her pleasantly.

'Oh yes, thank you. Where do they live?'

'Groningen—not far. I should be home about tea-time and we shall need to leave here about half past six.' He paused on his way to the door. 'Be careful if you go out—it's very cold and treacherous underfoot.'

'Yes, Radinck.' She smiled at him as she spoke and he came back across the room and kissed her hard and quick. Caroline sat a long while after he had gone trying to decide whether he had meant it or whether he was feeling guilty; she remembered all the books she had read where the husband had tried to make amends to his wife when he had neglected her by being kind to her, only in books they sent flowers as well.

They arrived a few hours later—a great bouquet of fragrant spring flowers; lilac, and hyacinths, tulips and daffodils, exquisitely arranged in a paper-thin porcelain bowl. The card said merely: Flowers for Caroline, and he had written it himself and scrawled Radinck at the end. Caroline eyed them at first with delight and then with suspicion. Was he, like the guilty husbands in all the best novels, feeling guilty too? She was consumed with a desire to find out more about the beautiful girl in Dordrecht. She was a satisfyingly long way away, but absence made the heart grow fonder, didn't it?

Caro spent the whole day vacillating between hope and despair, so that by the time Radinck came home she was in a thoroughly muddled state of mind—made even more muddled by his unexpected friendly attitude towards her. He had always—well, almost always—treated her with punctilious politeness, but seldom with warmth. Now he launched into an account of his day, lounging back in his great chair, looking to be the epitome of a contented man and even addressing her as Caro, which seemed to her to be a great step forward in their relationship. She went up to change her dress presently; it was to be a long dress occasion and she chose one of the dresses she had bought in den Haag. A rose pink crêpe-de-Chine, patterned with deeper pink roses, it had a high neck and long tight sleeves and the bodice was finely tucked between lace insertions. She swept downstairs presently, her mink coat over her arm, and then stopped so suddenly that she very nearly tripped up. She had never thanked Radinck for his flowers.

A deep chuckle from the end of the hall made her look round. Radinck was sitting on a marble-topped side table, swinging his long legs, the picture of elegance. 'Such a magnificent entry!' he observed. 'Just like Cinderella at the ball—and then you stopped as though you'd been shot. What happened?'

'Oh, Radinck, I remembered—I'm so sorry, I never thanked you for the flowers, and they're so lovely. I hope you don't mind—I put them in my room, but I'll bring them downstairs tomorrow...'

'I'm glad they pleased you.' He swung himself off the table and came towards her. 'That is a charming dress, and you look charming in it, Caro. I have something for you; I hope you will wear it.'

He took a box from a pocket and opened it and took out a brooch, a true lovers' knot of diamonds. 'May I put it on for you?'

He held the lovely thing in the palm of his hand and she put out a finger to touch it. 'It's magnificent!' she breathed. 'Was it your mother's?'

His hand had closed gently over the brooch and her fingers. 'No—I chose it yesterday as I came through den Haag on my way home. I want to give it to you, Caro, and I want you to wear it.'

She looked up into his face; his eyes were bright and searching and his brows were raised in a questioning arc.

'Why?' asked Caro, her head full of the girl in Dordrecht. Flowers, and now this heavenly brooch—it was even worse than she had thought, although Radinck didn't look in the least like a guilty husband.

'I'm afraid to answer that,' said Radinck surprisingly, and pinned the brooch into the lace at her neck with cool steady fingers.

And when he had done it: 'It's my turn to ask a question,' he smiled down at her. 'Why did you ask why, Caroline?'

Oh dear! thought Caro, now I'm Caroline again, and said carefully: 'Well, first you sent me those heavenly flowers and now you've given me this fabulous brooch, and you see, in books the husband is always extra nice to his wife when he's been neglecting her or—or falling in love with someone else—then he buys his wife presents because he feels guilty…'

He looked utterly bewildered. 'Guilty?' he considered it for a moment. 'Well, yes, I suppose you're right.'

Caro's heart dropped like a stone into her high-heeled, very expensive satin sandals. 'So there's no need to say any more, is there?' she asked unhappily.

Strangely, Radinck was smiling. 'Not just now, perhaps—I don't really think that we have the time— we are already a little late.'

She said yes, of course, in her quiet hesitant voice and got into her coat, then sat, for the most part silent, as he drove the Panther de Ville to Groningen, almost sixty kilometres away. The roads were icy under a bright moon, but Radinck drove with relaxed ease, carrying on a desultory conversation, not seeming to notice Caroline's quiet. He certainly didn't present the appearance of a guilty husband who had just been found out by his wife. Caro stirred in her seat, frowning. She could be wrong...

There wasn't much chance to find out anything more at the party. The ter Brinks were a youngish, rather serious-minded couple living in a large modern house on the outskirts of Groningen, and Caro found herself moving round their drawing-room, getting caught up in the highbrow conversations among their guests. She had met most of them already and almost all of them spoke excellent English, but—typical of her, she thought—she got pinned into a corner by an elderly gentleman, who insisted on speaking Dutch despite her denial of all knowledge of that language, so that all she could do was to look interested, say '*neen*' and '*ja*' every now and then and pray for someone to rescue her.

Which Radinck did, tucking a hand under her arm

and engaging the elderly man in a pleasant conversation for a few minutes before drifting her away to the other end of the room.

'My goodness,' said Caro, when they were safely out of earshot, 'I only understood one word in a hundred—thank you for rescuing me, Radinck. What was he talking about?'

Her husband's firm mouth twitched. 'Nuclear warfare and the possibility of invasion from outer space,' he told her blandly.

'Oh, my goodness—and all I said was yes and no— Oh, and once I said *Niet waar* in a surprised sort of way.'

Radinck's shoulders shook, but he said seriously: 'A quite suitable remark, especially if you sounded astonished. "You don't say" is an encouraging remark to make—it sounds admiring as well as astonished, which after all was what Professor Vinke expected to hear.'

'Oh, good—I'd hate to let you down.'

He had guided her to another corner, standing in front of her so that she was shut off from the room. 'I believe you, Caroline. It is a pity that you cannot return my opinion.' He took her hand briefly. 'Caro, perhaps I'm going away for a day or two. Are you going to ask me where and why?'

She stared down at his fingers clasping hers. 'No, I don't break promises.'

He sighed. 'Perhaps the incentive isn't enough for you to do that…'

And after that there was no further chance to talk. They were joined by friends, and presently Tiele and Becky came across to talk to them and although they left soon afterwards they only discussed the party on their way home. They didn't talk about anything much at dinner either, and afterwards Radinck wished her a cool goodnight and went away to his study. And yet, thought Caro, left alone to drink her coffee by the fire in the drawing-room, he had looked at her very intently once or twice during the meal, just as though he was wanting to say something and didn't know how to start.

She went to bed presently and made a point of being down in time to share breakfast with Radinck the following morning. It was hardly the best time of the day to talk to him, but she didn't feel she could bear to go on much longer without asking more questions. When he had read his post she said abruptly: 'I'm going to break my promise after all. Are you going to Dordrecht?'

Radinck put his coffee cup down very slowly. 'Why should I wish to go to Dordrecht?' His eyes narrowed. 'Ah, now I see—the flowers and brooch were to cover my neglect, were they?' His voice held a sneer. 'You really believe that I would go tearing off after a girl young enough to be my daughter, just like your precious novels?' He got to his feet, looking to her nervous gaze to be twice his normal size and in a very bad temper indeed. 'Well, Caroline, you may think what you wish.'

'When are you going?' she asked, for there seemed no point in retreating now. 'And you needn't be so very bad-tempered; you wanted to know if I was going to ask you where you were going, and now I have you're quite peevish…'

He stopped on his way to the door. 'Peevish? Peevish? I am angry, Caroline.' He came back to tower over her, still sitting at the table.

'And why do you keep on calling me Caroline?' asked Caro. She had cooked her goose and it really didn't matter what she said now. 'And sometimes you say Caro.'

He said silkily: 'Because when I call you Caroline I can try and believe that you are someone vague who has little to do with my life, only I find that I no longer can do that…'

'And what am I when I'm Caro?' she asked with interest.

'Soft and gentle and loving.' He bent and kissed her soundly. 'You have brought chaos to my life,' he told her austerely, and turned on his heel and went.

Caro sat very still after he had gone. Things, she told herself, had come to a head. It was time she did something about it. And he hadn't told her when he was going to Dordrecht, or even if he was going there. She poured herself more coffee and applied her wits to the problem.

She got up presently and went to the telephone. Radinck's secretary at his rooms was quite sure that he wasn't going anywhere, certainly not to Dordrecht, and at the hospital, in answer to her carefully worded enquiries, she was told that the Professor had a full day ahead of him. So he had been making it up...to annoy her? To get her interested in what he did? She wasn't sure, but his kiss had been, even in her inexperienced view, a very genuine one. Caroline nodded her mousy head and smiled a little, then went to the little davenport in the sitting-room and after a great deal of thought and several false starts, composed a letter. It was a nicely worded document, telling Radinck that since they didn't agree very well, perhaps it would be as well if she went away. She read it through, put it in its envelope and went in search of Willem, who, always willing, got out the Mini used by the staff for errands and rattled off to Leeuwarden, the letter in his pocket.

It was unfortunate that Radinck happened to be doing a round when Willem handed in his letter with the request that it should be delivered as soon as possible; the round took ages and it was well after lunch before a porter, tracking him down in the consultants' room, making a meal off sandwiches and beer, handed it to him. He read it quickly and then read it again, before reaching for the telephone. He had been a fool, he told himself savagely; Caro had believed that he had gone to Dordrecht because he had been attracted to that girl—and he shouldn't have let her believe that he had stayed there, either. He was too old to fall in love, he reminded himself sourly, but he had, and nothing would alter the fact that little Caro had become his world.

Noakes answered the phone and listened carefully to the Professor's instructions. The house was to be searched very thoroughly; he had reason to believe that the Baroness, who wasn't feeling quite herself, could be in one of its many rooms. Radinck himself would call at the most likely places where she might be and then come home.

He spent the rest of the afternoon going patiently from one friend's house to the next, calling at the shops he thought Caro might have visited and then finally, holding back his fear with an iron hand, going home.

Caro had been sitting working quite feverishly at her knitting for quite some time before she heard the car coming up the drive, the front door bang shut and Radinck's footsteps in the hall. It was a great pity that the speech she had prepared and rehearsed over and over again should now fly from her head, leaving it empty—not that it mattered. The door was flung open and her husband strode in, closing it quietly behind him and then leaning against it to stare across at her. Meeting his eyes, she realised that she had no need to say anything, a certainty confirmed by his: 'Caro, you baggage—how long have you been here?'

'Since—well, since Willem took my note.'

'The house was searched—where did you hide?'

'Behind the door.' She made her voice matter-of-fact, although her hands were shaking so much that stitches were being dropped right left and centre. She wished she could look away from him, but she seemed powerless to do so. Any minute now he would explode with rage, for he must be in a fine temper. His face was white and drawn and his eyes were glittering.

Caroline was completely disarmed when he said gently: 'I have been out of my mind with worry, my darling. I thought that you had left me and that I would never see you again. I wanted to kill myself for being such a fool. I had begun to think that you were beginning to love me a little and that if I had patience I could make you forget how badly I had treated you.' He smiled bleakly. 'I have just spent the worst two hours of my life…'

Caro's soft heart was wrung, but she went on ruining her knitting in what she hoped was a cool manner. 'I didn't mean you to be upset,' she explained gruffly. 'You see, I had to know…well, I thought that if you m-minded about me at all, you would look for me, but if you didn't then I'd know I had to go away.' She dropped three stitches one after the other and added mournfully: 'I haven't put it very clearly.' Not that it mattered now. He hadn't said that he loved her and everybody called everyone else darling these days.

Radinck crossed the room very fast indeed. 'Put that damned knitting down,' he commanded, 'you're hiding behind it.' She had it taken from her in a ruthless manner which completed the havoc she had already wrought, but it really didn't matter, for Radinck had wrapped her in his arms. 'To think that I had to wait half a lifetime to meet you and even then I fought against loving you, my darling Caro!' He put a finger under her chin and turned her face up to his. 'I think I fell in love with you when you told me to give you a needle and thread and you'd do it yourself…only I'd spent so many years alone and I didn't believe there was a girl like you left in the world.' He smiled a little. 'I carry one of your handkerchiefs, like a lovesick boy.'

He kissed her gently and then very hard so that she had no breath. 'My beautiful girl,' he told her, 'when I came in just now and saw you sitting there it was as though you'd been here all my life, waiting for me to come home.'

'Well, dear Radinck, that's just what I was doing.'

Caroline's voice shook a little although she tried hard to sound normal. 'Only I didn't know if you would.'

He kissed her again. 'But I did, dear heart, and I shall always come home to you.'

She had a delightful picture of herself, with her delightful children, waiting in the hall for Radinck to come home…and now she would be able to wear the pink organza dress. She smiled enchantingly at the idea and Radinck smoothed the mousy hair back from her face and asked: 'Why do you smile, my love?'

She leaned up to kiss him. 'Because I'm happy and because I love you so much.'

A remark which could have only one answer.

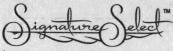

MINISERIES

National bestselling author

Debra Webb

FILES FROM THE COLBY AGENCY

Two favorite novels from her bestselling Colby Agency series— plus Bonus Features

Love and danger go hand in hand for two Colby Agency operatives in these two exciting full-length stories!

Coming in September.

Bonus Features include:

The Writing Life, Trivia and an exclusive Sneak Peek!

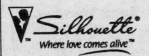

Where love comes alive™

THE FORTUNES OF TEXAS: Reunion

In September, look for...

Lone Star Rancher

by *USA TODAY* bestselling author

LAURIE PAIGE

Fleeing a dangerous stalker, model Jessica Miller retreats to Red Rock, Texas, to Clyde Fortune's ranch... the last place on earth she expects to find love. But when Clyde opens his home to Jessica, the brooding loner also finds himself opening up his heart for the first time in years.

Silhouette®

Where love comes alive™

SAGA

USA TODAY bestselling author

Dixie Browning

A brand-new story in
The Lawless Heirs miniseries...

FIRST TIME
HOME

Reeling from the scandalous ruin of her
career and love life, Laurel Ann Lawless
escapes to North Carolina and turns to
relatives she's never met. She soon feels
a strong sense of belonging—with her
newfound family and her handsome
new landlord, Cody Morningstar.

Available
in September.

Where love comes alive™

LAUNCHING AUGUST

Fall in love all over again with classic stories by *New York Times* and *USA TODAY* bestselling authors.

Fantasy by Lori Foster
Available August 2005

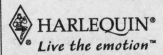

SHOWCASE